I0557021

# When the Truth
# is a Lie

Book One of *The Truth and Lies*
Five-Part Series

## Demetrice Nichele

Published by TJS Publishing House
PO Box 2382
Matthews, NC 28106
www.tjspublishinghouse.com
contact@tjspublishinghouse.com

Published in the United States of America
ISBN-13: 978-1-952833-35-9
ISBN-10: 1-952833-35-3

Fiction / African American / Romance
Fiction/African American/Suspense

# DEDICATION

I've been working on this book for a long time, and I could not have gotten it done without the strength of God. I have to thank Him for this blessing and the blessings to come. Next, I would like to thank my best friend, Petrina Winston, who is like a sister to me. I love our weekly conversations about life, with you living on the west coast while I'm on the east coast. We've been friends since the fourth grade, and no matter where we live and how much time goes by between our visits, we have always been able to maintain our close friendship for forty years. During one of our many conversations about life, you encouraged me to write a book. You reminded me of how much I used to write while in grade school. Thank you so much for reminding me of this gift. You are and have always been a great friend to me.

I would like to thank my children, Kyia Jones, and Tyshon Prezzy. You both are my heartbeats, and I am proud to say that you have grown to be genuinely good people. Thank you for always supporting and encouraging me in whatever I set out to do.

Last but definitely not least, my supporters Tekia Williams, Michelle Prezzy, Cheryl Daughtry, and Shirley Bray-Sledge. Thank you all for reading my book before it was published, giving me your input, and encouraging me to move forward. Also, to my Aunt Queen Mitchell, thank you for always having my back and being there always. To Sharon Battle, thanks for the endless love and support pushing me to get this book finished and published.

If I have left anyone out, please forgive me. I do love and appreciate you, also. Please charge it to my head and not my heart.

# ACKNOWLEDGMENTS

To my editor, Shameka Daughtry, who is also my sister, thank you so much for taking the time to read my very, *very* rough draft and correcting all of my errors, helping me to make it into a story that everyone can enjoy and understand. You are an awesome editor and sister!

Thank you also to my wonderful and funny publishing consultant Tonya Joyner of TJS Publishing House. She came in at the end, formatting and pulling everything together for me, and it has been a blessing.

Tessa walked into Pretty Plus Boutique and looked around in awe. She had officially started her own clothing line for plus-sized women almost three years ago, and business was continuing to boom. Who would have thought that the plus-size dress designs she'd had drawn in college would become a legitimate business? Then again, why should she be surprised?

Being a plus-size woman herself, she found that there weren't many places that catered to the curves of a woman of her build-- retailers who did carry plus-sized clothing didn't offer a big or stylish selection. She'd turned a negative into a positive-- serving the needs of the overlooked while building a brand and a name for herself.

She started her business by selling out of her home, and with the help and encouragement of her parents and sister, took a chance and opened the boutique. After nearly three years in business, she'd expanded her collections to include evening wear, swimwear, casual wear, and wedding dresses. With all of her success, she still couldn't believe that it all really happened-- her degree in fashion merchandising and design was worth every cent! Pretty Plus Boutique was a huge success. Not only did she have a storefront, but she had an online version of her boutique where people from across the country were able to purchase pieces of her collection. The doors of opportunity were open for her-- she'd even had the opportunity to travel to Los Angeles last year to design a dress for an up-and-coming plus-size actress who had heard about her work. At 35 years old, Tessa was on her way to living out her dreams.

Tessa grew up as what was considered to be chubby, but she never let her size make her feel inferior to the other girls in school. She grew up with two loving parents who had always told her that she was smart, beautiful, and that she had a good heart. Tessa's sister and best friend, Angela, who was two-years younger than her, was also beautiful and smart. Both women had cinnamon-brown complexions, and deep-set dimples in their cheeks-- compliments of their beautiful mother, Elizabeth Grant. Angela wore her hair short and stylish, while Tessa wore hers to her shoulders and curly.

Although Angela was not a plus-size woman, she believed that all women should feel beautiful and should not be limited in fashion because of their size. The two sisters became business partners, and together, they made the business blossom. Angela was great at handling the marketing and business aspects of the boutique. They had their sisterly disagreements, but they never let it interfere with business.

The phone rang as soon as Tessa walked through the door.

"Good morning. Pretty Plus Boutique, this is Tessa. How can I help you?" Tessa waited for the caller to respond to her greeting, but they hung up on her. She had been getting a lot of hang-up calls lately, but she didn't have time to worry about it.

"Good morning, Sissy!" Angela strutted into the store looking beautiful in her royal blue knee-length pencil skirt and her black peplum top, along with the signature four-inch stilettos that she never left home without. She sported her Gucci sunglasses, and she wore her short natural hair curly today.

Tessa smiled at her sister. "Good morning, sunshine! Aren't you in a good mood today? You must have had a good night." Tessa looked at her little sister with a smirk on her face.

Angela and her husband had been married for ten-years, and even with three children, they still acted as if they were newlyweds. She and her husband, Donte, married when they were just 22 years old, and Angela was pregnant. He treated her sister like a queen, and she treated him like a king. They were the perfect couple in Tessa's eyes, and she hoped to have the same type of loving relationship one day.

She had a feeling she was going in the right direction because Sam Thompson, the man she had been seeing for almost two-years, was truly making her happy. He repeatedly told her how beautiful she was, and they had so much fun together. He treated her well, loved her, and all of her curves. The thought of him made her smile. He was kind, giving, and very considerate, unlike her last boyfriend, David. David was abusive and could never keep a job. He only wanted to live off of her. He was the type of guy who thought she was

3

insecure about her size and that insecurity would make her accept his behavior. The turning point for Tessa was when he beat her because she wouldn't give him gas money to drive her car. She had forgiven him one too many times, and enough was enough. She had him arrested and kicked him to the curb.

Sam was the contractor who renovated her boutique. The moment she saw him, she was smitten, but she was careful to keep it all business. She thought he was flirting with her, but she wasn't sure. Trying to get her business off the ground kept her from dating much.

The phone rang again, and Angela picked up. "Pretty Plus, this is Angela." Angela began to smile and looked at Tessa. It must be Sam, Tessa thought. Angela confirmed when she handed Tessa the phone.

"Good morning, babe. How are you?" Tessa greeted Sam with all smiles. The sound of his deep voice made her melt. Sam was one of the finest, sexiest, chocolate men she knew, and he knew how to treat a lady.

"Good morning, beautiful. I just wanted to make sure you made it to work okay, and you really need to let me come and pick your car up to get a new tire. I'm not comfortable with you riding on that one, Tessa, especially when you stay at the boutique working so late at night."

Tessa smiled at how much she loved this kind, considerate man. "Baby, the tire is fine. I'll go and have it replaced when I get a break."

Sam persisted, "You are so hardheaded, Tessa.

Promise that you will go." Tessa laughed, "I promise, baby, and I will call you when it's done."

Sam didn't really want to let it go, as she was such a workaholic, but he gave in anyway, "Okay, darling, make sure you call me. Also, don't forget to check your calendar for our getaway to the Poconos. I know you like to be at the boutique on the weekends, but it will not hurt your business to be away for one weekend. You have to take time for yourself. Angela already told you she would be available to handle things. You need it, Tessa. You are going to burn yourself out at this rate."

Tessa sighed in defeat, "Okay, Sam, I will double-check with Angie and get back with you today. You're right."

Sam was happy that Tessa was finally seeing his way. "Okay, love you! Have a wonderful day, and don't forget to call me when you get that tire changed."

Tessa laughed, "Okay, babes. Enjoy your day." She ended her call and looked at her sister.

Angie just laughed and shook her head while walking to the back of the store, where their offices were. "Girl, you got it bad!" Tessa laughed. She wanted to agree with her sister but had no time to respond as her employees walked into the store. It was time to start opening.

# 2

Tessa looked around her spacious bedroom, making sure she packed everything for her weekend getaway with Sam. She was excited about going to spend some time with him, but at the same time, she was experiencing some anxiety about being away from the boutique for two days. She was sure Angie would be able to handle things, but Pretty Plus was her baby.

"Tessa, baby let's go!" Sam was waiting at the door, holding her luggage.

"Coming!" She walked out of the house to join her man, and they walked to his black Range Rover. He put her luggage in the back of the truck while Tessa waited patiently for him to open the door for her. They were officially on their way to their first weekend getaway. Tessa sat back and enjoyed the view as they drove from Virginia to the Poconos. During the drive, they passed the five-plus hours by talking about their businesses and future plans and goals. When they arrived at the resort, Tessa was amazed by the scenery that was laid out before her. They checked in, showered, changed, and had a romantic dinner. Afterward, they took a long stroll along the nature trail. It was relaxing. She'd needed this! Why had she denied herself this much-needed break for so long?

Later that evening, Tessa stepped out of the jacuzzi. She felt great! The Champagne Towers suite was amazing. The decor was cozy and romantic-- there was even a heart-shaped, heated pool in the suite and another fireplace in the sitting area. She gazed at the fireplace in their bedroom and admired the champagne glass jacuzzi that sat in the middle of the room. They had definitely enjoyed utilizing that!

Sam walked up and wrapped his arms around her, and started to kiss her neck. She immediately became excited. With Sam, she felt sexy and beautiful, "I love you, Tessa."

Tessa exhaled and enjoyed the affection. "I love you too, Sam." She turned around and kissed him deeply. Sam began to explore her body. He led her to the heart-shaped bed and climbed on top of her.

He kissed her all over her body. He made sure he loved every curve. She felt like she was going to explode. No man had ever made her feel so good. It wasn't just about the physical with Sam that made their lovemaking so intense, but it was also emotional. He took care of her heart and showed her every chance he got how much he loved her. He cared about her, and that made her attraction to him almost overwhelming at times. When it comes to her feelings for Sam, it felt as if she was falling off a cliff, and she couldn't stop falling. On her way down, she bypasses all of her past heartbreaks and fears, and she can't break her fall.

He spread her thighs and began to lick the folds of her vagina. Tessa braced herself because she knew what was about to happen. No matter how many times he did this to her, it always felt as if it was happening for the first time. Tessa began to squirm and gripped the sheets. She moaned out loud. This only encouraged Sam to spread her legs open and stick his tongue inside of her. Tessa could not take anymore. She screamed, "Sam, I'm cumming!" Sam applied more pressure with his tongue, and Tessa trembled and screamed even more.

When she finished, she breathed heavily. Sam kissed his way back up to her lips. He entered her and started to slowly move in and out of her, giving Tessa a chance to regain her composure. Tessa quickly began to grind, moving with his rhythm, and they both picked up the pace. Sam could take it no longer, yelling, "Tessa, I love you!". He exploded inside of her and rolled off of her.

They lay still for a few moments, both of them trying to catch their breath. Tessa looked over at Sam and smiled. She reached over and wiped the sweat off of his bald head with her hands. He looked so sexy with his chocolatey skin glistening and his muscular chest moving up and down as he tried to catch his breath. She reached out and ran her finger down the muscles on his arm.

Sam looked at her and smiled. "Tessa, I never met anyone that I felt so comfortable around. You make me feel so good, and your love is genuine. There isn't anything fake or superficial about you, and that's what drew me to you. You go out of your way to make me happy, and I do the same for you because your happiness makes me happy. Baby, I want us to build on this relationship and make it something special because you are special to me. When I'm away from you, I miss you so much. I don't want this to ever end." Tessa felt tears coming to her eyes. Could this be the man that God put on earth for her? She was overwhelmed with the love and happiness she felt at this very moment. She didn't want this weekend to end, but it had to.

Tessa was in her office working on some sketches for a wedding dress, but the dress wasn't for a plus-size bride. Tessa was tempted to turn down the woman's request, but Angie wouldn't hear of it-- especially since the woman had offered to pay almost double for what Tessa would usually charge for this type of dress. Angie warned her not to discriminate based on size, and if she could prove that she could create fabulous designs for all sizes, then there would be nothing in the way to expand the empire that they were trying to build.

She was meeting the client that day to show her the sketches that she had created based on what the woman described in their numerous emails. Rhonda, Tessa's salesperson, knocked on her office door before entering, "Sorry to bother you, Tessa. Your client's here." Tessa stood up and followed Rhonda to the front of the boutique.

When Tessa walked out front, she found a very pretty, very petite woman who looked as if she could have passed for a teenager. She had sandy-brow hair that flowed down to the center of her back, and her light skin made her hazel eyes stand out.

"Hi, I'm Tessa," Tessa mustered up the warmest smile she could while extending her hand out for the woman to shake, "I'm so glad to finally be able to meet you." Tessa took a glance at what the woman was wearing-- it was no wonder she was able to pay double the usual price.

The woman looked down at her hand for several long moments before she reached out and shook it. "Hello, I'm Yvette Duncan, and yes-- it is so nice to finally meet you." Tessa relaxed a little and led Yvette into her office.

"You can have a seat, Yvette." Tessa nodded towards several cushioned seats in front of her desk. Yvette glanced around Tessa's office and noticed the magazine covers and articles hung up around the room in reference to Tessa's designs and clothing line. "Can I offer you something to drink?"

"No, thank you, I couldn't help but notice that you have many representations of your work."

"Yes, I do," Tessa proudly answered, "I've been really blessed-- only been in the business for three years, and I've already designed for women all over the country who've had trouble finding clothes that complement their curves. That's why I was surprised that you want me to design your wedding gown because I don't understand why you would like a designer who specializes in the plus-size category when you are clearly not."

"I'm the daughter of Congressman Ed Duncan," Yvette started. "He raised me to help our own, so when we see a small business, we try to give them some recognition to help with their growth." Yvette had a proud smile on her face and a glint in her eyes that Tessa didn't yet understand, "I am not in the habit of doing things in the traditional way-- I want something different and edgy. I know that you usually do plus-sized designs, but I am challenging you to step out of your comfort zone and do something different. Ms. Grant, if you are not up for this project, I completely understand."

Tessa raised her eyebrows. She wasn't sure how to feel about this woman, who was sitting in her establishment, challenging her talent. Nonetheless, the customer was always right, "Ms. Duncan, I can assure you that I will have no problem providing you with the highest quality of service. Now, let's move over to the larger table, and I will show you what I've drawn up so far."

After an hour-long meeting, Tessa finalized the design that matched what Yvette was searching for. They talked for a while longer in order to get to know one another better-- Tessa found out that Yvette was Congressman Ed Duncan's only daughter. Yvette's fiancé, Charles, is a successful business owner who was mentored by Ed Duncan for several years. That's how they met.

She also learned that the Duncan family was well-known throughout the Tidewater community because of the work that the family has done-- this included funding different programs to help the low-income families of the surrounding area. Ed Duncan also donates and holds rallies in order to stop the violence in the tidewater area.

Margret Duncan, the wife of Ed Duncan. also heads many charities for the underprivileged families of the area and had also started a shelter for abused women.

Tessa thought that the opportunity to be able to design for the Duncan family was a blessing. Tessa has also come to the conclusion that Yvette was not as bad as she thought she would be, and she could picture the two of them becoming friends when this was over.

Tessa and Yvette both agreed to meet in a week for Yvette's final approval on the sketches. Yvette had given Tessa a deposit for half the cost of the dress, as she was impressed with the work Tessa had done so far.

## 4

Later that night, Tessa was relaxing in bed with Sam while watching a movie. Tessa felt herself dozing off. She had a long day. After work, she went over to Sam's place because he had prepared dinner for her. Now, they were relaxing after an intense love-making session. This was the perfect ending to a long day.

She was excited about her new client, but she kept it to herself. She wanted to be sure that everything went well before she shared the news with Sam. Tessa was kind of superstitious when it came to things like that. She didn't tell anyone unless the sale was final, as she feared she would jinx it.

Tessa dozed off, thinking about how perfect her life was turning out-- it seemed like everything was falling into place. She had a prosperous business, a loving family, a great home, and all her bills were paid, good health, and a man who treated her like the Queen she was. What more could she ask for?

The next morning, she got up early to go to her parent's house for breakfast. She made it her business to get up early each Saturday to eat breakfast with her parents. She loved them dearly, and there was nothing she wouldn't do for them.

Tessa's mom was a retired schoolteacher, and her dad was a retired police captain. After 31 years of marriage, her parents were still very much in love with one another. They lived comfortably in the quiet town of Jarratt, VA. Tessa lived an hour away in Richmond, but she made it her business to spend time with them at least twice a week. She seemed to look forward to it even more than they did.

Tessa pulled up to her parent's house. Her father was enjoying his morning ritual: sitting on the porch reading a newspaper and drinking a cup of coffee.

"Hey, daddy!" Her father stood up to greet his eldest daughter. George Grant was still a very handsome man and was still able to turn women's heads-- young and old.

"Hey, Baby Girl. How are you?" Tessa wrapped her arms around her dad. No matter what happened, he would always be the favorite man in her life.

"I'm good, Daddy. How are you feeling?" Tessa waited for his answer, but it was always the same. "I'm good, Baby Girl. No need to complain." Tessa walked into the house and straight to the kitchen to greet her mother. "Mommy, your favorite daughter has arrived." Elizabeth Grant was standing at the stove stirring the fried apples she was preparing for their Saturday breakfast. She turned around and smiled at her eldest child showing a beautiful deep set of dimples that she had passed down to her daughters. She was beautiful at 60-years-old. She had cinnamon brown skin, and beautiful salt and pepper hair that she kept pulled up in a bun most of the time.

The smell of bacon and cinnamon filled the air. "Hey girl, what's going on? I called you last night, but you didn't answer."

Tessa sighed. She'd told her mother time and time again to call her cell phone if she didn't answer the shop or house phone, but she refused. She knew if it was an emergency, she would call Angie and have her call Tessa on the cellphone. She didn't understand it, but who was she to question her mother? "Mommy, I stayed with Sam last night."

Tessa's mom raised her eyebrows, but she didn't say anything. She learned a long time ago to let these girls live their lives. They raised the girls to be smart, strong, respectable women, and they had yet to disappoint them.

She trusted their judgment, and only offered her advice when they asked for it. Tessa went on to tell her mother about her trip to the Poconos with Sam, and the things that went on that week at the shop. They discussed the holidays and plans to go shopping. Tessa left her parent's house feeling great. Her life was amazing. She was in good health, her business was booming, her family life was great, and she was in a loving relationship with her soulmate. She was truly blessed.

## 5

A week later, the day before Tessa was to meet Yvette for approval of her final sketches, she received a call from Yvette. "Hey, Tessa. Sweetie, how are you?"

Tessa smiled. "Hi, Yvette. I was just putting the final touches on the designs for you."

Yvette smiled. "Great! I was wondering if you could possibly come out to my home for our meeting. I have so many vendors to meet with this week; it will really put me off if I were to drive all the way to Richmond tomorrow. Of course, I would reimburse your travel cost in the final payment." Tessa agreed to go out to her home in Norfolk. She was actually curious to see where Yvette Duncan lived.

The next day, Tessa woke up early to start her day. She prepared herself for the long drive in traffic to the Tidewater area. After a two-hour drive, Tessa pulled up in front of the huge beautiful home with a manicured lawn. She gathered her belongings, walked up to the door and rang the bell. A pretty, young Hispanic woman answered the door in a maid's uniform.

Tessa was impressed. The maid led Tessa to the

immaculate and expensively furnished living room-
- the place where she told Tessa to set up.

After about 20 minutes, Yvette appeared. She
looked prettier than she did at their first meeting.
She was sporting a yellow jumpsuit and strappy
white sandals. Her hair was pulled up into a sloppy
bun which made her look even more youthful.
"Tessa, don't you look fabulous today! I hope you
didn't have any trouble finding the house. I am so
excited about today! You have no idea how anxious
I was last night. I could barely sleep. Have a seat
and let's have some refreshments before we get
started, girl."

The maid brought in a veggie platter, finger
sandwiches, and a fruit platter. Yvette offered Tessa
some wine, but Tessa asked for water instead. After
some small talk and refreshments, they got down to
business. "Tessa, this is just beautiful. I knew I
wasn't making a mistake when I chose you! I have
to have this dress. Did you bring the contract? I
want to sign on the dotted line!"

Tessa smiled. "Yes, I did! I am so glad you
approve." She pulled out the contract and began to
explain the terms. Yvette signed and Tessa was
officially her wedding gown designer.

This was the most money Tessa had ever made
in one order, and there was more to come once
Yvette's wedding photo was posted on the internet
and in the society papers. Tessa was giddy with joy.

"You know, Yvette, I think I will have a glass of wine after all."

Yvette smiled. "No, this is an occasion for champagne. I will be right back." While Tessa sat on the couch smiling, she heard footsteps behind her.

She was startled when a familiar voice said her name. She turned around slowly and to her surprise Sam was standing in front of her in an expensive business suit holding a Louis Vuitton briefcase. They both looked at each other in shock for a minute. For some reason, Tessa had a sick feeling in her stomach, but she didn't know why. "Sam, what are you doing here? And what do you have on?"

She was used to Sam wearing jeans and occasionally some khakis. He never wore suits. As a contractor, renovating and building, his days consisted of grungy clothing most of the time. Sam was at a loss for words, and before he could respond, Yvette came walking back into the room. "Charles, baby, when did you get here? Tessa, this is my handsome fiancé, Charles. Babe, this is Tessa. She is making my dream wedding dress." Sam stood still for a minute before he held his hand out to Tessa, giving her a pleading look. For some reason, Tessa reached out and shook his hand.

The room was getting hot, and Tessa felt as if she was going to be sick. She felt as if she was going to faint at any minute. Yvette handed the bottle of champagne to Sam. "Sweetie, open this and toast with us. We're celebrating the fact that I will have my dream dress, and it's all thanks to Tessa!" Sam grabbed the bottle from his fiancée and popped it open. Tessa jumped at the sound. She felt as if she was having an out-of-body experience. She wanted to jump up and run out of there, but she couldn't. She took the flute filled with champagne and sat down as she watched Yvette's lips moving but she just couldn't make out what was being said.

She drained the glass of champagne and she felt herself starting to come back. Yvette looked and frowned. "Tessa, are you okay?"

Tessa jumped at the sound of Yvette's voice. "Yes, I'm fine. Just a little tired. I have been keeping long hours lately."

Yvette smiled and walked over to her fiancé who was just standing there looking as uncomfortable as Tessa. "Well, please do take care of yourself, sweetie. I want you to be well so you can make my dream dress."

She wrapped her arms around Sam and gave him a long kiss on the lips. Tessa jumped up and began to gather her belongings. "Well, Yvette, I really need to get going. I have a very busy day and it's a long ride back to Richmond.

Sam finally found his voice. "Let me help you take your things to your car."

Tessa didn't answer. She couldn't even look at

Sam. She just wanted to get out of there as quickly as possible. Sam reached for Tessa's sketch pad and box of swatches. Tessa gave them to him and followed him to the front door. She stopped as if she forgot something and looked at Yvette. "Thanks for everything, and I will be in touch." Yvette smiled and crossed her arms.

"No bitch, I will be in touch. Charles, please escort this fat bitch to her car and tell her you never want to see her fat ass again." Yvette looked at both of them and laughed. "I wish I could have taken a picture of your faces when you all saw each other. Do you think this was all a coincidence? And Tessa, don't even think about backing out on making my dress. I signed a contract, and you accepted my money. I would hate to have to sue you and ruin your life and career. For the life of me, I still don't understand why you would cheat on me with her of all people. Frankly, I'm insulted! Do you really think I'm that stupid, Charles? All of your late meetings and all of the sudden you want to be so hands-on with your contracting business, when you have staff that does all the labor and dirty work. I also know about your little rendezvous with her in that Richmond apartment. You underestimated me Charles, and that was a huge mistake on your part."

Both of them just stood looking stunned. Tessa spoke first. "Yvette, I didn't know he was engaged. He told me his name was Sam. I had no idea. This is all a shock to me." Yvette rolled her eyes and glared at Sam who stood quietly holding on to Tessa's belongings.

"Well, now that you know, stay away from my man, Tessa. I mean it. I can make your life very miserable. And that's not a threat, it's a promise. I will leave you two lovebirds to say your good-byes. Charles Samuel Thompson, I will meet you in the bedroom. You have two minutes to wrap this shit up. Tessa, I expect to hear from you in two weeks to give me an update on my wedding gown."

Yvette walked out of the living room leaving Sam and Tessa staring at each other. Tessa quickly walked out the door and Sam ran behind her. "Tessa, I am so sorry! Please give me a chance to explain all of this." Tessa turned around and looked Sam directly in the eyes and slapped him with all of the strength that was left in her. Sam stumbled back and dropped her belongings. Tessa bent down and gathered as much as she could and threw it in her car. Sam bent down and tried to help her.

Tessa looked at him and held her hand up as if she was going to hit him again. "Stay the hell away from me 'Sam', 'Charles', or whoever the fuck you are!" Tessa drove away and she was finally able to let out her tears. She was so upset that she had to get off at the next exit to have a break down. Her cell phone rang, and she saw it was her sister. "Hey." That was all she could muster up.

Angie could immediately tell something was wrong. "It sounds like things didn't go so well." Tessa sighed trying not to speak much.

She couldn't talk and keep her emotions under control at the same time. "I will be at your house in two hours to tell you about it." She thought about Angela's husband and her nieces wandering around her house and changed her mind. "Better yet, meet me at my place in two hours."

Tessa didn't wait for her sister to respond-- she ended the call and tried her best to concentrate on the road back to Richmond.

## 6

Everything had gone according to plan. Yvette became suspicious of Charles six months ago when he suddenly started working long hours. He started staying in Richmond overnight because of some job that needed his attention. What really piqued her curiosity was his loss of interest in sex. Usually, Charles would practically beg her for some, and she would only give in to avoid an argument. She hated the way he would grunt and sweat all over her, making both of them all messy-- but, for the past six months he had become distant and was suddenly wrapped up in his business or a meeting with her father to help those people in the ghetto.

He would come home, shower and go straight to bed. At first, she was relieved, but soon she became suspicious. She immediately called a private detective to have him followed. She found out about the apartment he kept in Richmond, the weekend getaway with this woman, and the days and nights he spent with her at her place and his apartment. The biggest shock came when she met Tessa. How could he cheat on me with her? She had to be at least 300 pounds.

Charles was a good-looking man, he worked out

daily and it showed with his huge muscles and six pack. He was milk chocolate, had a neatly trimmed goatee and kept his head shaved bald. He looked really good for forty. What in the world did he want with this woman? Maybe it was the sex, but how could he even be attracted to her? Yvette cried many nights about this situation, but she refused to cry anymore. She came from a prominent family, and if this scandal got out then it would make her family a laughingstock.

Yvette refused to be a victim, and she wasn't going to let that heifer have her man. She and her family had invested too much into Charles. If it wasn't for her family, Charles wouldn't be where he is today. Her father was there for him when he and his sick aunt had no one else. She watched her father groom Charles from a ghetto thug into a successful black businessman. Her father noticed his potential and nurtured him to success. Ed Duncan is a man who always tried to help the underdog. He invested in Charles's contracting business and threw a lot of work his way; so much work that Charles had to hire crew to work with him.

Eventually, his business grew to a point where he acquired a large staff, and he did not have to do the physical labor himself unless he just wanted to be hands on. He had five crews that did all the physical work while he did the paperwork and contracted his crew out for work. He owed all of his success to Ed Duncan. Yvette returned from college and realized how both of them could benefit from being a couple. He was no longer the thug charity case that hung around her father. He was the kind of man she wanted in her life. Charles was kind, handsome, prosperous and easy going. He went along with anything she said, and she loved the feeling of control.

After dating for four years, she suggested that it was only right if he proposed to her. He agreed as usual, and they were planning the event of the year. Her parents couldn't be happier that she was marrying a good man like Charles. She refused to let this fat bitch ruin her life.

Charles walked in, disturbing her thoughts. "Listen Yvette, I know I was wrong."

Yvette held up her hand. "Save the apologies and excuses Charles. I've known about this for six months, but it ends today. You will not humiliate me or my family sneaking around with this dressmaker. You could have at least had the decency to cheat with someone on my level. Look at her! What?? Did you have a big girl fantasy or something? Never mind. I will give you a pass this one time. You better get your shit together. If it wasn't for my family, you wouldn't be where you are now. How dare you spit in my father's face and do something like this?"

Yvette knew she had him when she said that. The only person in the world he did not want to hurt or disappoint was her father. He had so much respect and love for her father, and her father felt the same for him. Charles finally spoke. "It's over between Tessa and I, Yvette. And no, I don't want to do anything to hurt you and your family."

Yvette smiled sweetly and walked over to him. "Good, now let's go on with our lives and put this mess behind us."

Charles put his arms around Yvette as she put her arms around his waist. Yvette was happy about how things had turned out, but she was no fool. That's why she had Tessa making her gown. She needed to keep her close to monitor what she was doing and make sure there was no funny business going on. She didn't want anything to ruin her big day.

## 7

Tessa cried her eyes out as she laid her head on her sister's lap. Her heart hurt so badly. She kept hoping that this was all a bad dream and that she was going to wake up at any moment.

Angie sat there quietly, stroking her big sister's hair, allowing her to cry. Her heart went out to Tessa. "Tess, just let it out, honey." Tessa sat up and wiped her eyes for what seemed like the hundredth time.

"Angie, what am I going to do? How could he hurt me like this? To make things even worse, I am designing and making the wedding gown for a woman who is marrying the man I love. The man who I thought I was going to marry."

Angie got up and poured a glass of wine before handing it to her. "Tess, we are going to figure this thing out. This bitch is either the evilest person alive or just crazy. Who does something like this? You told her you didn't know about her. Why would she want to make you suffer? And I can't believe that Sam didn't say a word."

Tessa sipped her wine and lay back on the couch. "Oh, he tried to talk to me when we walked out of the house, and I slapped the shit out of him."

Angie looked at her sister in shock and they both burst out laughing. Tessa laughed so hard thinking about how Sam fell back and dropped everything.

"Alright, sis, we have to figure things out. This is a mess, but we are going to get through this shit. That bitch has not won. I don't know what type of game she is trying to play, but we're not going to lie down and let her walk all over us. Tomorrow morning I'm calling our attorney to see if there is a way out of this contract."

Tessa panicked. "No, Ang! Word of mouth is the best advertisement. I can be blackballed! No one will want to do business with me. I have to do this. There is no way out unless they call off this wedding." Tessa's eyes began to water again as she thought about Sam and the situation.

Angie sat down next to her sister and rubbed her back. "Tess, you need some answers from Sam. I think the next time he calls; and he will call, you need to hear him out. I'm not a big fan of Sam right now, but I can read people pretty well and he was not faking his feelings for you. I don't know what happened and how you guys got in this situation, but I feel in my heart that he really loves you. You deserve some answers and Sam is the only one who can give them to you."

Tessa didn't respond. She just closed her eyes tightly and prayed for this nightmare to end.

## 8

Charles stood looking at himself in the mirror as the tailor measured him for his tux. He had the worst headache and felt like the scum of the earth. He missed Tessa like crazy, and she was not taking his calls. How did he allow all of this to happen? When he met Tessa, she was shopping for a contractor to renovate her shop. He was immediately drawn to her upbeat personality and positive outlook on life. She was a smart, independent, hard-working woman who was starting her own business.

No, she was not the typical model type, but she was beautiful to him. He could not stay away from her. It was like he was drawn to her. She was so warm, down to earth, and funny. They had so much fun together. It felt so normal to be around her. Her family was also so warm and welcoming-- just like the Duncans, with the exception of Yvette.

It was like a breath of fresh air to be around Tessa. He cared about Yvette, but he wasn't in love with her. Yvette's father had been good to him. He believed in him when no one else would. He owed Ed Duncan his life. When he agreed to marry Yvette, he felt as if he had no choice-- Yvette hinted on several occasions that it was expected because they were dating. He pretty much let Yvette have her way because of her father, but now he realized how miserable he was. He felt hopeless and there was no way out. He just didn't know what to do about this situation.

He'd hurt Tessa in the worst way, and he just wanted to go to her and make things right-- but, he was stuck.

Rome had been sitting with Charles for about thirty minutes watching him look off into space as if he'd just lost his best friend. He placed his hand on his shoulder. "What's up, man? You're a million miles away." Charles looked at his best friend Rome. He was the only one who knew everything that was going on. He trusted Rome with his life.

He shook his head and responded to Rome "I just can't get her off my mind."

Rome patted his friend on the back. "Man, that's because you're in love with that woman. You don't have to do this, man. Talk to the old man and let him know how you feel. I'm sure he wants his daughter to marry someone who's in love with her and not someone who feels obligated."

Charles shook his head. "No, I let it go too far. I shouldn't have agreed to marry her, and I shouldn't have dragged Tessa into this mess. It's all on me, man."

Rome stood in the mirror as the tailor began to

measure him. "Shit happens man, and everybody makes mistakes. You got caught up. Whatever you do, I got your back, but I think you should follow your heart. You only live once. Tessa is cool. I can see why you're feeling her so much."

Charles smiled. "Yeah, she is."

Rome handed Charles his phone. "Give her a call from my phone, man. Maybe she will pick up. Say what you have to say to get her to listen or meet with you." Charles grabbed his friend's phone and dialed Tessa's number.

## 9

Tessa finally went back into the store after taking two days off. She knew she could not hide forever. She just hadn't been feeling well, but she knew it was the stress of everything that had taken place. She couldn't eat, sleep, or concentrate and she had been getting headaches.

She put on some makeup and clothes before dragging herself to work. She greeted her staff and went straight to her office, closing the door once she was inside. As much as she was trying to get back to normal, it was going to take some time. Her heart was broken, and she had never felt so much pain in her life. She felt as if she'd never get over this. She hadn't had the strength to work on the wedding dress for Yvette, but she knew she had to. She decided to go out and work the floor with the girls. It would be a welcomed distraction from sitting alone and thinking.

As Tessa was busy ringing up a customer's purchase, the phone rang. She picked up on the first ring. "Pretty Plus Boutique. This is Tessa."

Sam spoke nervously. "Tessa, I know you don't want to talk to me, but please don't hang up. I just need to talk to you. I just want you to hear me out.

Please just agree to meet me so we can talk. I know I don't deserve your time, but please just hear me out."

Tessa sighed. She didn't know what to say. She did want to hear him out. She did still love him, but she was so hurt. "Sam, I don't know. What if she has you followed?"

Charles thought for a moment. "Let me worry about that. Just say you will see me." Tessa agreed. Charles felt relieved. "I'll come by your place. I will have my boy Rome drop me off." Tessa hung up the phone and went back to her office. She needed a moment, and she called Angie to tell her what just happened.

That evening, Tessa sat nervously on her couch and waited for Sam to come over. She was still angry with him, but she also missed him, and she needed answers. She heard a knock at her door and her stomach dropped. She walked over and opened the door for Sam. She looked at him and fought the urge to put her arms around him. She studied his face. He looked tired and sad.

*Snap out of it Tessa*, she had to tell herself-- he's a liar and a cheater. She stepped away from the door and went back to sit on the couch. Sam took that as an invitation to come in. He walked in and sat next to her on the couch. Tessa looked straight ahead as she was the first to speak. "You said you were going to give me an explanation. I'm listening."

Sam was caught off guard by her abruptness. He

cleared his throat and turned to face her. "Tessa, I know there is no excuse for what I've done to you. I met you and I was immediately drawn to you. I didn't expect it to go this far. I thought we were just going to be, you know, cool. I came to your boutique to give you an estimate and we began to talk, and I really enjoyed talking to you. I found myself finding reasons to call you. It had gotten to the point where I decided to work on your shop personally, just to get a chance to see or talk to you. I know it sounds crazy. I fell in love with you Tessa, everything about you. I know I should have told you about Yvette. It's just that I guess I got caught up. My relationship with Yvette isn't the same as ours."

"I don't feel the same way when I'm with Yvette as I do with you. Yvette's father was there for me during my lowest point. I wouldn't have this successful business if it wasn't for him. I wouldn't have been able to give my aunt the best of care before she died if it wasn't for him. When I started dating and having sex with his daughter, she started talking about marriage. At the moment, it seemed like the right thing to do. I'm not in love with Yvette. I'm in love with you, Tessa." Sam held his head in his hands as the tears rolled down his face.

Tessa looked over at him and her heart felt like it was breaking in a million pieces once again. "Sam, you really hurt me. You weren't honest with me. I went over to you and your fiancée's house, and the rug was pulled right from under me. I'm not going to sit here and act as if I don't love you, because I do. Your selfishness put me in a dangerous position. Your fiancée could have done anything to me in her home. I am now in a contract and designing a wedding gown for her to wear to become your wife! How do you think that makes me feel? I know I'm not the ideal size, but I am a woman, a good woman and I didn't deserve any of this, Sam. You said you love me, but you're marrying another woman! How is that so? I don't think you know the meaning of love. Please leave, Sam."

Tessa got up and went to her bathroom and left him sitting on the couch. Charles walked to the bathroom door and spoke to her through the door. "Tessa, I didn't know what love was until I found you. I am so sorry for hurting you. I promise I will figure out a way to make this right. I do not want to let you go. Just Yvette is talking to him; give me some time. I will fix everything."

Tessa felt as if her head was going to explode, and she felt dizzy. "Sam do not make things worse. I could lose everything because of you. Please, just leave me alone."

Sam stood at the door and listened to the woman he loved cry. He held his hand up to the door for a moment, before letting himself out. When Tessa heard him leave, she began to cry even louder. Her heart was telling her to run behind him, but her brain was telling her to let him go and to move on.

## 10

Yvette sat in her bedroom, waiting for Charles to finish dressing to escort her to a dinner party. He was over an hour late. She called off the private detective because she felt as if she got her point across to the both of them. With Tessa designing her gown, she would be able to keep tabs on her as well. Charles had been quiet but behaving and attending to his duties as normal. She watched him as he began to undress and walked out of the bathroom with a towel around his waist, never once looking in her direction. This infuriated Yvette. She walked up to him, waiting for him to turn around and acknowledge her presence.

Charles turned around and looked directly into her eyes, but he didn't utter a word to her. He was so confused about his emotions and did not want to say the wrong thing to her. He knew he was wrong, but he felt her actions did not help the situation. At this point, he did not know what he was going to do about the situation. He loved Tessa with all of his heart, but he didn't realize the extent of his love for her until he saw the hurt in her eyes. It felt like someone had taken a knife and plunged it in, his heart.

As he looked at Yvette, he realized she was about to become his wife and it was all out of obligation and gratitude, but not love. Her father had been the father he never had, and while he cared about Yvette, he wasn't in love with her. Something was missing in their relationship, but he never had the courage to express this to her or risk his relationship with her father. Now he was looking at this woman scorned; and he could tell by the look in her eyes that she had no intention of losing him to Tessa.

"Charles, we need to talk." He sat back down on the bed. He took his time to finish drying off his body. He was not looking forward to this conversation. Yvette sat on the bed and waited patiently for her fiancé to join her. When he walked over to the bed, she stopped him and removed his towel from around his waist. She dropped down to her knees and took his soft penis into her wet mouth. Charles held up his hands to protest but the feeling was too good. He could feel himself begin to get hard.

She ran her tongue over the head of his hardness and began to suck with such force that it made his legs weak, and he began to moan. He reached down to grab her head, but she slapped his hands away. Charles felt tears come to his eyes as his body betrayed him. He could feel himself about to cum, and he expected Yvette to pull away. She never allowed him to cum in her mouth, but she didn't she began to suck even harder. "Oh, shit!" Charles screamed before filling Yvette's mouth with his seed. He was amazed at how she was taking it. She had never done that before. When he finished, he fell backwards on their bed, breathing hard.

Yvette jumped up and ran into the bathroom and he could hear her rinsing and gargling as if she had poison in her mouth. She walked back out and stood over him with her hands on her hips. "By the way you enjoyed that, I think I can tell exactly what Tessa was doing to keep you going back to her. Even though it makes me feel dirty, that's a sacrifice I will make to get you to stop this bullshit. As far as I'm concerned, it's over with you and her, and she will be out of our lives soon enough after the wedding. I expect you to be the respectful, devoted man that you promised me that you would be, Charles."

"I won't tell my parents about your shenanigans, and I have called off the PI. But don't get it twisted; I won't hesitate to put him back on your ass as soon as you give me a reason to. And I will make sure my father blackballs and ruins your ass. Now let's get ready to go to this dinner party and act like the power couple we are. My parents are back in town, and they will be there. Don't you dare disrespect, or embarrass me, like that again." She leaned over and kissed him on the lips and walked into the bathroom to freshen up her makeup. Sam sighed heavily and looked up at the ceiling. What in the world was he going to do?

## 11

Charles stood off to the side dressed in his black Tom Ford suit, pulling at his tie. He really hated these functions. Tonight, the tie around his neck felt like a noose and he just couldn't seem to get enough air. He was on his 4th drink and the scotch was not easing his nerves at all.

Yvette was walking around putting on airs, as usual, all dressed up in her Versace cocktail dress, flawless makeup, and $300 hairstyle. She took pride in giving off the appearance of a cultured, rich, proper debutante. Little did everyone know she had just finished sucking off her cheating fiancé and was in the process of blackmailing the woman he was cheating with.

Yvette looked over at him with a strange look on her face. It was as if she could read his thoughts. He held up his glass to her and smiled. He was finally feeling the effects of the scotch and he didn't want the feeling to end. "Charlie!" Ed Duncan walked up and patted Charles on his shoulder. Charles smiled widely. Regardless of him hating his daughter at this very moment, he was still very fond of Ed.

"Welcome back old man!" The two men

embraced one another. One would think they were really father and son. "How was Europe? Where is Ms. Maggie?" Charles looked behind Ed expecting to see his wife walking up behind him.

"She's at home. I think she has a touch of jet lag. How's it going? How is the wedding planning going? In a few weeks you will legally be a part of the family!" Charles felt his stomach drop at Ed's words. He smiled.

"Well, you know how it is. I told Yvette to just let me know the time and place and I will be there." Both men laughed.

"Where is my little girl, anyway?" Charles shrugged.

"She's around here somewhere, networking or socializing." Ed looked at his future son-in-law. He had known this young man for a very long time, and he was like the son he never had. They were very close, so he could tell that something was bothering him.

"Look, I'm about to leave so I can go check on my wife. Why don't you walk me out?" Charles looked relieved for the chance to get away from that place, if only for a few minutes. He followed Ed out to his car. The two men walked out into the spacious courtyard taking the long way to the valet. Charles inhaled the fresh air. "So, Charlie, what's going on with you?" Charles stopped in his tracks and thought of how to answer Ed's question. He knew if anyone would know his mood, it would be Ed Duncan-- the man practically raised him.

Charles met Ed at a mentoring program that his aunt put him in when he was fifteen, after both of his parents died of drug overdoses. Charles was getting into a lot of trouble because he felt alone in the world. It was Ed who saw the potential in him and took him under his wing. He took time with him and showed that he cared. He took him to his mansion and let him sit at his dinner table with his wife and daughter, even though he was a parentless kid from the ghetto. He treated him like a human being. Ed never gave up on Charles.

Ed believed Charles was someone special even when he didn't think he was. His business was a success because of Ed and his connections. Ed had groomed him to be a good man. He taught him if you don't have pride, dignity, and self-respect then you don't have anything. How could he tell him what he had done to his daughter?

Charles looked at his mentor and friend and was speechless. Ed smiled and put his hand on Charles's shoulder. "I think I know what is going on and you don't have to be scared to tell me. We all went through this, man." Charles looked at him confused.

Ed smiled and motioned for him to join him on the bench in the courtyard. "Every man gets nervous and stressed out before taking that big leap. Your life isn't going to be the same. Instead of just worrying about yourself, now you have to worry about her and her feelings and what's best for the marriage. Marriage is a whole lot of work, and it isn't just about sex and love, man. No more staying out late with the fellas, no more bitches and no late-night partying. Hell, I can't even take a shit with the door open!" Charles laughed out loud. "Don't worry man, believe me all of those fears and anxiety are going to leave your body once you see your beautiful bride walk down the aisle. Did you guys make the appointment for counseling with the Pastor?"

Charles shrugged and felt the anxiety again. He wished for another drink at the mention of talking to the Pastor. "I'm not sure, sir. Yvette is handling everything."

Ed stood up. "Well, I'm going to ask her about it because that's very important. Reverend Reynolds won't marry you guys without him counseling you all first to make sure you're ready for marriage. Let me get home to check on Maggie." Sam nodded and stood up to walk Ed to retrieve his car from the valet.

## 12

Tessa sat in her office, staring at the final changes she had made to her drawings for Yvette's gown. She sighed and told herself not to cry anymore. She told herself that this was just business, and that Sam did not exist anymore. She wished that her brain would tell that to her heart.

As she stood to get some fabric from her worktable, the room began to spin and she stumbled. Her sister walked in just in time to grab her and keep her from falling.

"Tess, what the hell?" Tessa immediately sat down in the chair near the table and took some deep breaths. Angie grabbed her bottle of water off of her desk and handed it to Tessa to drink.

Angie rubbed her sister's back. "Tess, I know it's easier said than done, but you have to take better care of yourself. You have a business to run-- plus, mommy and daddy are worried about you. Your skin is pale, you barely eat, and now I walk in here and you were about to faint. You're losing weight rapidly-- I'm calling the doctor to have you checked out."

"No, Angie. I'm going to be okay. I just forgot to eat today. I've been so busy. I promise I'm getting better each day."

Angie looked at her sister and wanted to cry. She wished she could take her hurt away. "Tess, when do you go see that bitch again?"

Tess sighed. "I go Friday to get her approval for the final sketches."

Angie frowned. "You're not strong enough to travel all the way to the Tidewater area. I'm going to call her and ask if she can come this way. It's not breaking the contract and I don't want that bitch to ever think she is calling all the shots!" Tessa just sighed again and smiled weakly at her sister. Her mom had raised two strong-willed women and at this moment, Angela was the strongest. Tessa was just going to let her take the lead. She just didn't have the strength to fight her and Yvette.

"Ok, that's fine with me."

Angie walked over and hugged her sister. "Don't worry Tessa, we are going to get through this, and you are going to be just fine. Now grab your bag, we're going to get something to eat, and I'm not taking no for an answer." Angie stood at the door and waited for Tessa to stand up to make sure she was steady and could walk on her own. Tess knew that Angie was watching her, so she stood up and held herself steady. She walked over to the desk and grabbed her purse.

She took a deep breath and thought to herself, it had been a month since she heard from Sam. She couldn't help but wonder if he was thinking about her. She felt her eyes begin to water and shook it off. She looked and smiled at her sister-- she followed her out of the boutique and to her car.

Later that week, Tessa sat nervously in her office waiting for Yvette to arrive. She walked into the boutique as if she owned it. She wore a mint green backless halter dress that stopped just above her knees and hugged her petite frame and added on a pair of gold strappy sandals. Her long hair was pulled up into a sloppy bun, and a pair of Gucci sunglasses rested on top of her head.

Angela had been awaiting her arrival and walked over to her when she entered the boutique. Yvette studied Angie as she walked over to her. It was hard to believe that she and Tessa were sisters, because while Tessa had a pretty face, she was overweight. Angie was petite and pretty as she wore a burnt orange jumpsuit that complimented her small frame, and her short haircut was styled in a cute bob. She had the same deep dimples in her cheeks that Tessa had and that made her even prettier. Being the professional she was, Angie smiled a fake smile as she approached Yvette. Even though she wanted to run up and open up a can of whoop ass on this bitch. She will never understand why the woman always blamed the other woman instead of the cheating man.

"Hello Ms. Duncan, how are you today?"

Yvette was taken aback by Angie's politeness. "I'm great considering I had to take this long ride down here."

Angie smiled sweetly. "Well, thank you for being flexible. Please follow me. Tessa is waiting for you."

As the two women entered the office, Tessa sat at her workstation patiently waiting. Last night, she made up her mind that she was not going to give this situation any more of her tears. She went and got her hair, nails and make-up done this morning. She also got a massage. It made her feel a whole lot better. She was dressed in one of her creations, a wine maxi dress that accentuated her curves, and a pair of Prada black pumps. Her makeup and hair were flawless, and her deep dimples made the smile on her cinnamon brown face even prettier. Her presence gave off a strong air of confidence and that infuriated Yvette and made Angie proud.

"Hey, Yvette, thanks for agreeing to come to me this time. Please have a seat!"

Yvette was speechless. She did not expect Tessa to be so cheerful. It almost made her wonder if she and Charles were still sneaking around. She made a mental note to check that out. "Well, hello, Tessa. I figured I would come your way this time. I can understand why you may not want to come back to our home." Tessa stared at her for a moment and decided not to entertain that statement but chose to just get down to business.

"I've made all of the changes you requested and I just need you to approve the fabric I've chosen to move forward on starting the gown." Tessa placed the sketch of the gown in front of Yvette.

Yvette studied the sketch and she had to admit she was impressed with what she saw but she wasn't going to say it out loud to these bitches. "This is good, now where is the fabric?"

Angie snickered because she knew this bitch loved the sketch and it was killing her to see that her sister was this good considering the fucked up circumstances. Tessa was proving that she wasn't going to let anyone, or anything destroy what she built. Tessa handed her the swatch of the fabric she had chosen. Again, Yvette loved it, but she did not say it. "This fabric will make the dress beautiful, and it will be able to hold the beading you wanted added."

Yvette fingered the fabric and nodded her head. "Are you sure it will be ready in time? I don't need our special day, or your reputation ruined because I don't have a gown."

Tessa smiled, again, showing those beautiful dimples. That was beginning to make Yvette sick to her stomach. "The gown will be ready in two weeks, and I will call you for an initial fitting. The final alterations will take a week. You will have your final fitting and upon your approval you will have your gown several days before your special day."

Angie sat back loving this exchange. She stood up and decided to help her sister out because she was sick of this bitch. "Tessa, if you're done and if everything meets your approval Ms. Duncan, I will need you to sign off on this document stating you are permitting Tessa to move forward with making the gown using this fabric and design." Yvette looked surprised that these women had their shit together. She snatched the pen and document from Angie and skimmed through and signed it. Angie took the document and handed it to Tessa. Tessa took the document and smiled. "Okay, now that we have that out of the way, please follow Angie out to the dressing room and my assistant seamstress will take your measurements. After that, you are free to go."

Angie ushered Yvette out of Tessa's office without Yvette or Tessa saying anything else to each other, and that was fine with Tessa. She sat down at her desk and took a sip of her bottled water and smiled. She couldn't believe she made it through without any drama. She was grateful for her sister, because she did not think she would have been able to do it without her.

She went to stand up and the room began to spin, she quickly sat back down. She frowned and thought to herself, she might have to go to the doctor because this dizziness was beginning to happen too often.

## 13

Charles sat behind his desk and shut his eyes. He had the worst headache and he had to go with Yvette to this counseling, but he just wasn't feeling it. Ever since this situation with Tessa happened, Yvette had become very clingy, and it was making him go insane.

He looked in his desk drawer and found some Tylenol. He took two, hoping this would give him some relief. He got up and headed out the door to meet Yvette for their first counseling session with the pastor. Once in his Range Rover, he rolled down the windows to let some fresh air into his lungs. The ride was 30 minutes, but he wished it was longer. He walked in the church and felt a sense of dread. Yvette had already advised him of what not to say, not that she had to. He had no interest in discussing his infidelity.

Reverend Reynolds and Charles walked at the same time. They exchanged pleasantries and the Reverend ushered them into his office. Once inside, he asked them how the wedding planning was going. Yvette lit up and began to go on and on. He didn't pay attention until she mentioned going to the boutique to get measured for her gown. It made him think of Tessa. He thought about calling her on several occasions, but he knew she would not answer. He thought of going to her house again, but decided against it. He finally decided to give both of them some time because he didn't know how to handle his feelings right now. He wasn't even sure if he was doing the right thing anymore.

Charles looked over at his pretty fiancée as she went on excitedly about the wedding. He really felt like an asshole because he didn't share her joy. He actually wished he was sharing this moment with Tessa. He loved sharing things with Tessa. She was always so supportive and always showed interest in what went on in his life and his business. And he was always excited to hear about her accomplishments. They pushed each other to be all that they can be. They would just lay in bed for hours talking about what they wanted in the future and the plans they were making to accomplish it.

He even shared with her the details of his childhood and how even now, he would sometimes lay in bed crying about his parents. Tessa listened and always told him that he was never alone because his parents were still in his heart. She would tell him how proud they would be that he didn't go down the same road as them. She even told him that it was a possibility that they had to die to save him from following in their footsteps. She always had a way of making sense out of things that didn't make sense to him.

The pastor began the session with prayer and the questions began. Charles answered saying what he thought was the right thing to say. When it was over Yvette seemed pleased and so did the pastor. Sam was just glad to get out of there. After his parents died, his faith hadn't been very strong. "Hey babe, do you want to go get a bite to eat?" Yvette grabbed his hand and asked him. That was the last thing he wanted to do. "No, my head is killing me. I just want to go to the house and get some rest; I have a busy day tomorrow." Before she could protest, he kissed her on the cheek and opened her car door for her. She got in and drove off pissed. Charles didn't care, and he knew it wasn't over.

Yvette made it home in record time. Charles was acting distant and strange, and she was going to get to the bottom of it. She really had been trying. She was doing things to him sexually that she would never do. What the hell was his problem? All he cared about was that stupid business. He even wanted to bring that talk into their bed at night. She politely told him their bedroom is not the place to discuss work and he should leave all of that talk at the office or call her father.

She was going to call the PI tomorrow to investigate Tessa and have him check up on Charles just to be on the safe side. She took off her clothes and heard Charles enter the bedroom. She smiled at him and decided to give him a chance to redeem himself. "Come join me in the shower, babe." Charles started to protest but thought about the wild sex they had been having and changed his mind. He was still a man and he figured he had better get it while he can because he was sure this would not last for long. He undressed and followed her into the shower.

## 14

Tessa sat in Dr. Anderson's office waiting patiently for her to enter. She wanted to find out the cause of these dizzy spells. Her obesity was an invitation for hypertension, diabetes and heart disease. If that was the case, she knew she would have to change her eating habits. She felt like it was stress and so did her mom. She really hadn't been eating and working on that godforsaken gown was enough to make her have hypertension. She just wanted it to be done so she could go on with her life. Sam had stopped contacting her and she was glad because she felt that each message he left declaring his love for her was just making her weaker. She had no intentions of being anyone's side chick or mistress. She was not cut out to be number two.

Dr. Anderson walked in and gave Tessa a warm smile. She had been her family's doctor since she was a little girl. "Hi, Dr. Anderson. What's going on with me?"

Dr. Anderson looked at her and smiled again. "The question is, what have you been up to lately?" Tessa began to worry, and she frowned. "Tessa, your blood pressure is elevated, but it's not that high that I will put you on meds. Not yet anyway. I want you to change your diet to a low sodium diet to try to keep you off the meds. With you being pregnant and all."

Tessa felt as she was going to pass out. "What did you just say to me?"

Dr. Anderson looked at her and smiled. "You're pregnant, girl!"

Tessa burst into tears. "No, this can't be happening-- not now. Not now!" Dr. Anderson put her arms around Tessa while she cried even harder. What was she going to do?

## 15

Sam was at the bar drinking and shooting pool with his best friend Rome. He and Rome grew up together in the projects and remained best friends and tight through all of the craziness of their childhood. Like Sam, Rome grew up with a drug addicted mother, but his father was doing a life sentence for murdering a police officer. The guys grew up as brothers and always had each other's back. Rome didn't have a mentor like Ed Duncan to steer him in the right direction, so he didn't have anyone to right his wrongdoings. This resulted in him getting an eight-year sentence in prison for robbery.

Sam stuck with his friend through the whole ordeal by visiting him and making sure he had money on his books. When he was released, Sam had just opened his contracting business and it was very successful. He immediately gave Rome a job. Rome had been gainfully employed ever since. He was able to get his mom into rehab and take care of her when she completed her program.

Rome always told Sam that he saved his life. "Bruh, how long are you going to walk around looking all sad?" Rome grabbed the pool stick and walked over to the table to make his shot.

Sam took a sip of his beer and shook his head, "I just don't know what I'm doing anymore, Rome. I feel like this whole thing is going to end really badly." Rome took his shot and sat back down with his friend at the table. "I saw Tessa the other day at the mall. I took my mom shopping for a birthday gift, and I ran into her. She looked great, man. She was made up all pretty, but her eyes were really sad."

Sam felt his stomach drop, "Why are you just telling me this? What did she say? Did she mention me? Was she alone?"

Rome smiled at his friend and shook his head. He and Tessa hit it off as soon as Sam introduced him. Tessa was sweet, down to earth, and nonjudgmental. Sam lit up whenever he spoke about her or was around her. While big girls weren't Rome's thing, after meeting Tess you could easily fall in love with her. She was definitely a great woman. He told Sam a long time ago he needed to end whatever he had with that spoiled, bourgeois, uptight Yvette to be with his soulmate Tessa.

He understood his friend's loyalty to Yvette's dad, but he also had to be happy. Rome hardly hung out with Sam when Yvette was around. He could tell that she did not approve of their friendship because of his background and where he lived. And that was fine with Rome because he didn't approve of her stuck-up ways. Sam was his friend, his brother and he would support him regardless of what decision he made.

"She didn't mention you man. She basically said hello and made small talk with my mom and kept it moving. It was almost like she wanted to walk away before she or I had a chance to mention you." Sam looked down at his beer and sighed heavily. He didn't know how to feel about what Rome had just told him. "Look Sam, you know I'll be there for you regardless of what you decide, but I really think you should take some more time to think things through. You were wrong for what you did, but just look at how Yvette is handling this whole thing with Tessa. Something is wrong with that broad. Any other woman wouldn't want the woman her man cheated with anywhere around. She got Tessa making her wedding gown! I just have a bad feeling about her and always have."

Sam had to agree with Rome, the wedding was coming up in a matter of weeks. How was he going to back out now? Her parents had already paid for the wedding and the honeymoon to Hawaii. Maybe he would have a talk with Yvette tonight. She would definitely be up waiting for him, asking for every detail of his night with Rome. She had already texted him three times asking what time he would be getting home.

## 16

Tessa sat in her parent's den feeling defeated, angry, and overwhelmed at the same time. She called Angie and told her to meet her at their parent's house because she wanted to discuss something with the family. Angie sat across from her sister looking worried. She thought Tessa was getting better but looking at her sister today, it looked as if she had a setback. She was hoping Sam's fiancé hadn't done anything else to her.

Elizabeth walked in with a tray of pound cake and George followed behind her with a pitcher of lemonade. They sat it on the coffee table, then sat down to join their daughters. Tessa cleared her throat and began to speak. "I know you guys are wondering why I called this meeting today. I have been going through a very emotional ordeal and I really didn't want to worry you guys with the details of my relationship issues."

Elizabeth was instantly worried. "Tessa, what's going on? Is everything ok with you and Sam?"

Tessa took a deep breath trying to fight back her tears. "No, things are a mess, Mommy. I found out that Sam is engaged to one of my clients."

Elizabeth jumped up and went to hug her

daughter. "What do you mean engaged, Tessa?"

Tessa pulled away from her mom because her embrace was bringing her closer to tears. "Mommy and Daddy, Sam, who also goes by Charles, is engaged to my client Yvette Duncan. She sought me out and hired me to humiliate me because she found out her fiancé was involved with me. Of course, I had no idea about any of this. I signed a contract and I have to make her wedding dress for their wedding. And the kicker is that I just found out that I am pregnant with Sam's baby. I'm pregnant, Mommy! I'm pregnant with Sam's baby and I don't know what to do!"

Elizabeth and Angie hugged Tessa. George sat quietly taking it all in. Angie had filled them in on the details about Yvette Duncan weeks ago, but she asked them to wait for Tessa to tell them. The part about the baby only added to his emotions and how he felt about Sam at this moment. He decided now was not the time to reveal his true feelings and what he wanted to do to Sam. He allowed his wife and daughter to comfort his baby girl. It hurt him to see her hurting like this.

Elizabeth began to rub Tessa's back and wipe her face with a tissue. "Baby girl, I know it doesn't seem like it at the moment, but everything is going to be okay. God does not make mistakes. This baby is your blessing in disguise."

Tessa looked at her mom in disbelief. "How do

you figure that, mommy? I'm not ready for a baby! I wanted to have a husband or man in my life before I became a mother. This is a mess! How am I going to run a business and take care of a baby? Let's not disregard the fact that this baby's father is about to be married to someone else!"

Elizabeth looked at her daughter with sympathy in her eyes. "Tessa, everything happens for a reason, and I will not have you trying to turn this new life you're about to bring into this world into something negative! We have too much of that going on now. Your father and I raised you girls to be strong, independent black women. There are millions of single moms raising more than one child and juggling careers. You're not the first and you definitely won't be the last. You won't be in this alone. You have a family to help you. You and that child will be just fine."

Tessa looked across at her father who had been silent during this whole exchange. "Daddy, I guess you're disappointed in me, huh?"

George walked over and grabbed his daughter's hand, kissing it. "Baby, I am always proud of you. You have shown me nothing but strength during this whole ordeal. Many women wouldn't have been able to continue to do business with that woman after what had gone on, but you're a trooper and the Lord knows this about you. That's why he has given you this blessing, to make you stronger. I know that you will make the right decisions for you and my grandchild. I will be right there to support you. As for the father, we will deal with that issue another time because the way I feel right now, I know I need to pray, or your Daddy might end up in jail."

"George, please do not talk like that! Violence is never the answer and whether you like it or not, he will be our grandchild's father. We have to figure out how to get along and what's best for this child." George didn't respond to his wife because he knew she was right, but as a father he felt like Sam needed to be dealt with.

Angie agreed with her mom, but had some reservations about if Tessa should reveal her pregnancy to Sam. She feared how his fiancée would handle the news and try to make Tessa's life miserable. Lord knows Tessa did not need any more stress. "Tess, do you plan on telling Sam about the baby?" Angie asked.

Tessa sighed. She was so tired of feeling sad and stressed. She was tired of these emotional rollercoasters she had been on, and she knew in her condition this was only the beginning. "Sissy, to tell the truth I haven't even thought that far. I'm just basically taking one day at a time. The first thing on my agenda was telling you guys and now that I have done that, I'm not sure what to do next."

Angie hugged her sister. "Well, take your time to figure things out. Tessa, we all love you and support you. We will be there for you all the way. Let me know if you want me to be there when you talk to him. You will make it through this, Sissy. I will be at every doctor's appointment from now on and make sure you take care of yourself!"

Elizabeth stood up. "I will also be right by your side. You will be just fine, baby. You will see. I'm not saying there won't be any rough times, but you will be able to overcome it all."

Tessa smiled at her family. She loved them so much. She would never be able to get through any of this without them and she knew that. Her next step was to figure out how and when she would tell Sam. She felt sick to her stomach just thinking about him and his upcoming nuptials and the part she was forced to play in the whole thing. She placed her hand on her belly and said a silent prayer asking God to give her the strength and knowledge to get through this and to make the right choices.

## 17

Yvette sat in Charles's home office using his computer to do some online shopping for their honeymoon. She decided to pull up Sam's email just to see what he had been up to. He had no idea that she knew his password. She frowned as she came across an email he'd sent to Tessa a few weeks ago. She felt her blood pressure rise as she read this email from her fiancé professing his love to another woman and how he never meant to hurt her and how much he missed her.

Yvette wanted to scream, but she knew that wasn't going to help her situation.

Reading a little more, she saw that Tessa didn't respond, but that wasn't enough for her. She wanted them both to pay. How dare he try to make a fool of her again? After all her family had done for his ungrateful ass. She texted him and told him she needed him to come home immediately.

He was out with that thug Rome. She told him time and time again that it wasn't a good look to socialize with the help. Five minutes after she sent the text he came walking through the door.

He called out for her, and she told him she was in his office. He walked in and looked at her strangely. She could tell that he was drunk. "Charles, how many times do I have to tell you not to drink and drive?"

He chuckled a little and dropped down on the couch in his office. "You just like to have all of the control, don't you? I'm a grown ass man, Yvette. I don't need you to tell me how to run my life." Yvette looked at him and rolled her eyes, she had no time to have this drunken conversation with him. She got up to walk out of his office. Sam jumped up and grabbed her arm. "What the hell are you doing in my office? I hope you found what the fuck you were looking for."

Yvette snatched away from him and sucked her teeth. "Take your fucking hands off of me! Don't you dare try to make it seem like I'm the fucking problem. You're the one that was running around with some obese seamstress! Is she on your level? Is that why you love her so much?"

Sam began to laugh. "Am I on your level, Yvette? Who the fuck is on your level? Here you are so busy trying to front for the public and caring so fucking much about image, you never take time to figure out who I really am, nor do you know who you are. You walk around all entitled with your nose in the air, not even bothering to realize what is going on. Outside of your shopping, extravagant trips, dinner parties and eating at these fancy ass restaurants, you have no idea what the fuck is going on."

"Not once have you even bothered to ask me how my business is going or even try to assist me and your parents in the mentoring program. Sure, you show up at the fundraisers acting like you care and like you're trying to help raise money to help the community, but the truth is you couldn't care less about these kids or the community because you never had to live that life. You don't have an ounce of compassion for any of our people or their struggle because you never had to struggle and it is eating you alive because all your life you have gotten every fucking thing you wanted and now you have no control over my..." Sam suddenly stopped his rant, realizing he may have said too much.

Yvette raised her eyebrows "Go ahead 'Charles', 'Sam' or whoever the fuck you call yourself, finish your statement. I have no control over your love for that fat bitch? Is that what you were going to say? Well, let me say this. I may not have any control over who you love, but I have control over who will fuck me over and make a fool out of me. And another thing, don't blame me because my parents were smart enough to get out of the ghetto and not get strung out on drugs. I don't owe anyone anything for living a good life, and you or no one else is going to make me feel guilty about it".

She walked out of his office and marched up the

stairs to their bedroom. She picked up the paperwork she received from the PI that morning, and after that conversation with Charles, she figured out what to do with the last bit of information she received from the PI.

## 18

After a long restless night, Sam woke up and got ready for his meeting with his future father-in law and the committee for the mentoring program. They finally found a building for another youth center for inner city kids in the Tidewater area along with an extension for an outreach program for teenage parents. This program was to be headed by Maggie Duncan and Yvette, but Yvette had yet to show up to any of the meetings or even show any interest in getting the program up and running.

Sam had already put together a team to start the renovations, and Ms. Maggie was about to plan another fundraiser to get her part of the program started. Rome was also an active member of the committee and always volunteered his services when needed. Sam and Rome arrived at Ed Duncan's office at the same time. They both walked into the office feeling the effects of too much drinking and too little sleep that morning.

Ed Duncan greeted both men warmly and ushered them into his boardroom. Ed Duncan was a very powerful man in that area. He owned several businesses that generated a lot of jobs in the community. He was actively trying to find ways to eliminate poverty in the low-income areas by providing resources and education to the youth and helping the elderly. He was responsible for many programs, especially feeding the hungry. Ed was also responsible for the homeless shelters that opened up in the community. He had regular meetings with law enforcement and his committee to ensure the police were doing what they were supposed to do, which is protecting and serving the community.

Ed was a hands-on activist for the community and the citizens loved him. His wife was his right hand. She was there with him all the way, helping and supporting his activities to help the community. For the life of him, he just couldn't figure out how their daughter ended up the way she was. Ms. Maggie walked in and gave out hugs to the committee. She was such a sweet, kind, classy woman, but she could also get a hood if the situation required it. She sat down and looked at Sam and asked, "Where is 'Vette? Is she on her way?"

Sam felt uncomfortable, but he answered anyway. "She left out early this morning saying she had some wedding details to take care of and she would try to make it afterwards. I thought she called you."

Ms. Maggie smiled and didn't respond. She almost looked embarrassed at her daughter's blatant distaste for helping the community. It was really starting to get to her. She made a mental note to contact her daughter and address her concerns with her about this and other issues.

## 19

Yvette sat in a park in Richmond waiting for the other person to join her in this little meeting she requested. She looked at her watch and began to get angry. He was fifteen minutes late and he hadn't even bothered to contact her to let her know he was running late. Maybe this was a sign that she needed to rethink this whole thing. She thought about the embarrassment her fiancé had caused her and pushed that out of her mind. She was doing what she had to do to protect her life and her family's investment.

Just as she was about to call to find out if he was going to show up, she noticed this fine specimen of a man walking towards her. He wasn't the type that she would take home to her parents, but he was sexy as hell. He had a bald head and a Hershey chocolate complexion. He wore a wife beater and a pair of jeans that hung off his waist with a pair of timberland boots. He had a scar on his cheek, but it added to the sexiness. He also had muscles bulging everywhere.

She remembered the picture the PI gave her and she knew immediately that this was Tessa's ex, David.

He walked up to her with such confidence and didn't crack a smile. He stopped in front of her as she stood to greet him. She held out her hand "David, I'm Yvette." David looked down at her hand, but he didn't take it. He looked directly into her eyes and didn't say a word. This unnerved Yvette and forced her to look down.

"Where do you know me from, and what you want with me?" David was standing so close to her, that she could smell the sweat on his body, and it was turning her on.

It was hard for her to concentrate. "Well, David, as I stated on the phone, I have a business proposition that I think you would be very interested in." David got even closer in her personal space, and she was beginning to feel a little fear.

"Who the fuck are you lady, how the fuck you get my number and how the fuck do you know me or what I am interested in?"

Yvette cleared her throat and tried to find her voice. "Like I stated earlier, my name is Yvette and I know your ex, Tessa." She saw his eyes get dark at the mention of Tessa's name. She knew she had to speak quickly to try to turn his mood around.

"Tessa has been having an affair with my fiancé and refuses to let him go. My fiancé has told her time and time again that he made a mistake and to leave us alone and she refuses. She has had my fiancé arrested for hitting her in retaliation for him not wanting her. We had the charges dropped but now she has made threats to me, and I am very fearful that she will carry out those threats. My fiancé and I work very hard, and we both are very successful and accomplished."

"I'm not from the streets like Tessa, and I feel as if she is bullying me and my fiancé. I had someone run a check on her and he came across some information stating that she had you arrested for the same thing as my fiancé. My fiancé never put a hand on her so I figured she must have done the same thing to you. I figured if I reached out to you, we could both get together and figure out a way to make her pay for making us miserable. Like I stated before, we are well established financially, and I can make this well worth your while."

David didn't say anything at first, but she could tell he was taking in everything she had said to him. "Yeah, Tessa did a nigga wrong, but I don't know what you want me to do about your situation."

Yvette smiled. She knew she was about to reel him in. "Well, I was thinking she cost my fiancée and I a lot of money in legal fees trying to clear his name, and if I'm not mistaken, you can't get a good job due to the conviction." David raised his eyebrows and this time he actually smiled and what a sexy smile it was! Yvette felt a tingle between her legs.

"Damn, you really did your homework. Yeah,

that bitch ruined my life. I'm staying at my cousin's crib until I get straight."

Yvette smiled, "Well, David, I think we can help each other out. Let's hit Tessa in her pocket like she hit us. It's come to my attention that she doesn't have any surveillance cameras in her shop. What if suddenly there is a break in at Pretty Plus and all of her beautiful merchandise is totally destroyed along with the shop? Maybe even a fire. I did some research and there have been a lot of break-ins and vandalism in that area."

David looked at Yvette, he was impressed, "You sure you're not from the streets? And who do you think is going to risk their freedom just to destroy her shop?"

Yvette placed her hand on his muscular arm, "That's where you start to benefit from this whole thing. How about you think about it and give me a call back. If you decide to make it happen, I'll give you $25,000-- half when you call me, half when the job is done."

David sat quietly and studied her to see if she was serious. Yvette decided to give him some reassurance. "Look David, I don't know you, and for me to contact you and make this offer out of nowhere lets you know that I am serious about this whole thing."

David rubbed his bald head while thinking, "Well, I need an incentive today to prove that you're serious."

Yvette began to think. She really didn't have a lot of cash on her, and she wasn't about to give him a check to create a paper trail. "I'll tell you what. I have another appointment here in Richmond in about an hour. How about I give you a call after my appointment, and we can meet again, and I will have $5,000 cash for you to show you that I am dead serious. Is that enough of an incentive for you?"

David's eyes lit up. That was music to his ears. "Okay, that'll work. Hit me up after your appointment and we can link up. That doesn't mean I accept your offer, it just means that I will think about it, babe." He smiled at her and walked away without giving her a chance to respond.

## 20

Tessa was exhausted. She had been up most of the night putting the finishing touches on the gown. Between morning sickness, lack of rest and the stress of her situation, she just didn't know how she made it through each day. If it weren't for her parents and Angie, she didn't think she would make it. She finished the gown and waited for Yvette to arrive for the final fitting. Angie just called and said she was running late and stuck in traffic. She almost panicked, because she didn't want to face this chick alone. But she had to do what she had to do.

Yvette walked through the door, and it took everything Tessa had not to roll her eyes at this bitch.

"Hi Yvette, I have everything waiting for you in dressing room one. Janet will assist you with putting on the gown. Just stick your head out and let us know when you're ready for her assistance." Yvette didn't even bother to speak. She just walked into the dressing room. That suited Tessa just fine. She just wanted to get this over with.

"Sorry Sissy, traffic is crazy!" Angie rushed into the shop out of breath. Tessa was relieved to see her sister.

"It's cool. The client is trying on the gown as we speak." Angie nodded and walked behind the counter to gather up some paperwork.

Yvette walked out in the gown-- Tessa had to do a double take herself. She looked stunning in the gown. The beading was perfect, and it was a perfect fit. Tessa stood back as her assistant seamstress handled Yvette in the gown. Tessa did not want to touch her. Angie walked over and was the first to speak, "It looks great! Tessa, you really did your thing. It looks like it's a perfect fit, also."

Yvette was speechless. She had to admit the gown was breathtaking and she looked beautiful in it. "Yes, Tessa, you did a really good job. 1 must say 1 am satisfied. Charles won't be able to take his eyes off of me when he sees me in this gown, and it's all because of you."

Tessa smiled, "Yes, I have been called a miracle worker."

Angie could not hold in her laughter. She wanted to go over and give her sister a high five for that one. But she remained cool. Yvette caught the dig and chose not to respond. She figured she would have the last laugh. Angie decided to try to wrap this little meeting up, "Well, Yvette, if you're satisfied with everything, we will send the gown to be professionally cleaned and have it to you in about a week." Yvette agreed and signed the document Angie gave to her stating that she was satisfied.

Tessa felt a sense of relief that she was almost done with the wedding business, but she still had to deal with Sam and telling him she was pregnant with his child. She decided to put in a call to Rome and ask him to have Sam contact her. She really didn't want to have this conversation, but she knew she had to tell him.

## 21

Yvette left Tessa's boutique feeling excited. In spite of everything that was going on, she felt good about the way things were turning out. She knew it just killed Tessa that she had to create such a beautiful gown for her to marry the man she was in love with. She couldn't wait for Charles to see her in it and with all she had planned for him on their wedding night, he would forget all about Tessa. For the life of her, she still could not understand how Tessa was pulling all of these good-looking men. First David, then Charles. She must really be a freak as big as she is.

Yvette pulled in front of the bank and parked. She needed to run in and get this money for David, so they could put this plan into motion. Just as she was about to step into the bank, her phone rang; it was her mother. She hit ignore. She would have to call her back after she finished taking care of her business.

Yvette withdrew the money and called David. He picked up on the first ring, "Yeah, where are you at?"

She was caught off guard by his abruptness. "I'm on my way back to the park. Can you meet me?"

"Yeah, I'm already here. Put it in an envelope and drop it in your purse and leave your purse unzipped", and he hung up just like that.

Yvette made it back to the park in twenty minutes. She walked quickly to the meeting place and immediately spotted David. David quickly walked over to her and grabbed her in his big strong arms. Yvette felt like she was going to melt and yet she was also confused. David bent down and kissed her deeply, shoving his thick tongue into her mouth. Yvette closed her eyes and began kissing him back before she realized it. David kept his mouth on hers. "I'm about to stick my hand in your purse to get the money out." That brought Yvette back to reality, and she felt embarrassed.

Next thing she knew, he had his hands running down her back, cupping her ass. It felt so good she let out a moan. He had his tongue in her mouth again kissing her deeply before he abruptly stopped. She was swooning. She opened her eyes. David was standing in front of her smiling. "I'll be in touch in a day or so to let you know what's up, ma." He walked away. Yvette stood there a minute, stunned. She got herself together and walked quickly to her car thinking to herself, *what have I gotten myself into?*

## 22

Tessa sat in her living room feeling nervous and sick to her stomach at the same time. She got a call back from Rome telling her that Sam would be coming through this evening. She made sure her hair was done and she put on some makeup to cover the dark circles forming under her eyes. She had on a simple red maxi dress she designed and some white flip flops. As each moment went by, she became more and more nervous. She had already thrown up and she was starting to feel flutters in her stomach. Her doctor had informed her to expect the feeling; it was the baby moving.

She smiled every time it happened. The thought of a human being growing inside her warmed her heart, regardless of the circumstances. She began to believe what her mother said about the baby being a blessing in her life. She just needed to overcome some obstacles and that process would begin in a few minutes. Tessa heard a knock on the door, and it made her jump. Her stomach began to flutter like crazy. Did the baby feel what was about to go down? She rubbed her stomach and walked slowly to the door. She opened the door and smiled at the sight of Sam. He looked so good and sad at the same time.

Part of Tessa wanted to run into his arms to hold him and never let him go, but she reminded herself of his lies, deceit, and how he was going to spend the rest of his life with another woman.

"Hi, Tess." He stood there and stared at her. She looked so beautiful, almost as if she was glowing. He wanted to give her a hug, but he wasn't sure of how she would receive it.

"Hello Sam," Tessa stepped away from the door to allow him to walk in. "Thanks for stopping by. Can I get you something to drink?"

Sam smiled and sat on her sofa. It felt good to be back in her presence. "I'll take a beer, if you have any." She walked off to the kitchen and grabbed one out of the fridge. She'd have to make a note to get rid of the alcohol in the house. No point in adding misery to misery. She was a nervous wreck, and she wasn't sure that she could get through this. She wished she could have a glass of wine to calm her nerves. She walked back in the kitchen, handed him the beer and sat across from him on her loveseat. They sat there and stared at one another for a few minutes. She wanted so badly to kiss him and to feel his arms around her, but that wasn't what this meeting was all about. Sam decided to start the conversation.

"Tess, you don't know how happy I was to hear that you wanted to see me. I feel like this meeting is long overdue. I am so sorry for my actions. I had no intentions of hurting you. We just clicked, and I found myself wanting to be with you all the time. I felt like we were kindred spirits. I kept telling myself that I was going to come clean, but time just went by so fast, and I just didn't want to risk losing you by telling you the truth. I know I was being selfish, but I fell deeply in love with you. I never wanted to hurt you and I felt like a real piece of shit after what went down at the house. You are a phenomenal woman, and any man would be lucky to be able to spend his life with you. I know I fucked up, Tessa. Hell, I feel fucked up. I just wanted you to know that I love you very much and I am truly sorry for what I've done to you. This engagement to Yvette is not what it seems. There is so much more to this, and I'm afraid if I go into detail, you really won't respect me. I feel like a piece of shit."

Tessa finally spoke after several long seconds. "Try me. You owe me that much. Tell me what your relationship with Yvette is all about."

Sam nodded his head and took a long sip of his beer. "I met Yvette when I was a teenager. Her dad was my mentor and still is my mentor. He practically saved my life. My parents were gone. I felt alone in the world. I only had my elderly aunt Hannah, and her health was failing. I had given up hope and started to get in trouble. My social worker

had my aunt sign me up to this mentoring program--
Ed felt I was too gifted to go down the wrong path
and I needed help. Ed chose me out of a crowd of
boys playing basketball. He talked to me every day
and was interested in my hopes and dreams. He let
me spend weekends at his mansion, took me
fishing, and taught me how to play golf. After a
while, I started going on family trips and spending
holidays with his family. My aunt became really
sick, and Ed paid for her care until the day she died
when I turned 20. I was already away at college,
because he insisted that I go to college to have a
brighter future."

Sam looked at Tessa and continued. "He took
care of all of my aunt's funeral arrangements, so I
did not have to worry about anything. By the time I
returned from college, Yvette was away at college.
We really didn't spend too much time together. I
became interested in renovating and building things
even though I went to school for business. Ed
noticed my gift of fixing and building things and set
me up with a job for one of his contractor friends.
The next thing you know I was taking jobs on the
side and getting more work than I could handle
alone."

"Ed helped me set up shop, and before I knew it,
I had a staff. I had become a successful
businessman and I was good at it. When Yvette
came home from college, I guess my success made

her see me in a different light. All of a sudden, she wanted to hang out with me or surprise me at my office with lunch. I was flattered, but she really wasn't my type. I would have told her that, but Ed and Ms. Maggie seemed so happy that we finally hit it off."

"I didn't have the heart to tell them that I wasn't interested. I didn't want to offend her or her parents. They had been so good to me. So, one thing led to another and next thing you know I'm engaged, and this huge extravagant wedding is being planned. Then, I met the love of my life, and I just didn't know what to do. I was caught up and I handled everything totally wrong and hurt someone very special to me."

Tessa felt tears running down her face. Should she tell him or just let him go? This was all too much for her. She still loved Sam, but everything was such a mess. "Sam, I'm not going to sit here and act like I'm over you and I'm okay, because I'm not. You hurt me more than David did! Do you know how bad and broken I felt listening to this woman, who I thought wanted to do business with me, insult me? Do you know how stupid I felt to know she invited me into her home under false pretenses? And the names she called me, you just stood by and allowed it to happen. I might sound crazy, but I don't want to believe that everything we had was a lie. I even questioned myself wondering if you were real, or did we really happen. Then reality sets in when I get emails from your fiancée listing her demands for her wedding gown I am being forced to make. It makes it all too real for me, Sam. You say you love me, but yet you're marrying another woman."

"I forgive you, Sam. Not because you deserve it, but because I need to move on with my life. I have so many great things coming, and I don't want to block my blessings hating you or Yvette. I wish you both happiness and I will pray for you both."

Sam sat staring at the floor speechless. He didn't know what to say, but he was glad she said she forgiven him. "Tessa, I thank you for your forgiveness and I hope one day you will find a man who deserves you."

Tessa got up and smiled. "Thank you, Sam. And thanks for coming over and giving me closure".

Sam got up and walked towards the door, Tessa closely following behind him. Once at the door, he turned around, took her into his arms and kissed her all over her face. When he reached her lips, he didn't hesitate to ease his tongue in her mouth.

Tessa didn't resist-- it felt so good! After the kiss, they stood there and held each other for a few moments. They knew this was the end, and they didn't want to let go. Sam kissed her again and this time his hands started to roam all over her body. He missed her curves. Tessa felt that familiar wetness between her legs she usually gets when Sam touched her. Her brain was telling her to stop, but her heart was telling her *one last time*.

She reached down and began to stroke the bulge between his legs, she knew there was no turning back now. She took Sam by the hand and led him to her bedroom. They were all over each other. Tessa felt like she could barely breathe.

Sam pulled her dress down, pulled down her bra cup and took her swollen nipple into his mouth. Tessa began to moan. She was so turned on. Sam let go of her nipple and pulled her dress all the way off, along with her bra. "You are so fucking sexy, Tess."

Tess smiled and started undressing him. She unbuttoned his shirt, and he helped her by taking it off along with his wife beater. Tess couldn't resist touching his muscular chest and licking his nipples. It was his turn to moan. Tess reached for his belt buckle and began to undo it.

When she was done, he unzipped his pants and stepped out of them. His cock was pointing straight out of his boxers and that made Tessa moan. She reached down and began to stroke it. Sam pulled her hand away because he was about to come and it was too soon. He grabbed her panties and pulled them down-- Tessa stepped out of them. He gently pushed her back on the bed and lied beside her. He took her nipple in his mouth again and began to rub her pussy. It was so wet and it was making him harder.

Tessa began to squirm and moan louder. He slid two fingers inside of her and began to slide them in and out of her. "Shit, Sam, you're going to make me cum!" Sam smiled down at her-- he couldn't believe how wet she was. He took his fingers out and placed them in her mouth so she could taste herself, she eagerly sucked his fingers. Sam got up and placed her legs on his shoulders.

He got on his knees and began to lick her wet pussy. He licked and sucked her clit while sliding his two fingers in and out of her. Tessa couldn't hold back any longer. She began to scream" Sam, I'm cumming!" Sam began to work his fingers in and out of her faster as he flicked his tongue over her clit. Tessa screamed and a burst of fluid shot out of her.

Sam didn't give her time to breathe; he stood up, lifting her legs even higher, and slid his hardness inside of her. "Shit, Tess, your pussy feels so good."

He began to work his dick in and out of her. With each stroke, he was hitting her G-spot. He knew she was going to cum again real soon. "Sam! It feels *so* good! Please, don't stop!" Sam began to grind his dick inside her and move his hips from side to side. This drove Tessa crazy. Sam knew her body and knew just how to please her. She began to scream, "Fuck me harder, baby!" Sam picked up the pace and began to stroke harder.

He leaned over and looked in her eyes. "Come with me, sexy." Tessa began to tremble and scream.

They both began to cum together. When they were finished Sam pulled out of her and helped her to get comfortable on the bed. He laid behind her and pulled her closer to him. Tessa began contemplating telling him about the baby. Deciding to, she turned around and faced him. "Sam, I have something to tell you." Just as she was about to tell him her phone started to vibrate.

## 23

Yvette walked into her parent's mansion and was greeted by their maid Ethel. "Hello, Miss Vette. Don't you look pretty today?" Yvette smiled and gave the older lady she had known all of her life a hug.

Miss Ethel was no joke. She worked for her parents for over 30 years. She demanded the utmost respect. She was a part of the family. If she saw Yvette get out of line, she didn't hesitate to set her straight, and it was done with her parent's blessings. So, Yvette learned at an early age not to play with Miss Ethel. She smiled at the woman who was considered to be her second mom. "Thank you, and you are looking beautiful, as usual."

Ms. Ethel blushed, grabbed her hand and led her upstairs. "Yo mama in her room getting dressed to go out to Sadie's house. It's a shame what happened to her boy. I feel so bad for her. I'm in here cooking a bunch a food to send by yo mama and daddy. She don't need to worry about feeding those other children with all of this going on. I tell you, I pray every day for these kids. The white folks killing them and then they killing each other."

Yvette was quiet. She had not heard anything

about what happened. She had been so wrapped up with her problems. As a matter of fact, she couldn't stay long at her parents' house-- David contacted her and agreed to do the job. She needed to talk to her mom about getting an advance on her monthly allowance. She would get an advance on her credit card for the rest and worry about explaining the bill to her parents later. She would just tell them it was for something for the wedding. She walked in her parents' large bedroom and called out to her mother. "Ma, are you in here?" Her mother called out from her walk-in closet that stored hundreds of outfits, designer bags and shoes. Yvette loved her mother's closet and used to spend hours in it when she was younger playing dress up. She spent even more time in it as a teenager trying to borrow something or another.

Maggie Duncan was in her sixties but looked like she was in her forties. She and Yvette could pass for sisters. She even had the same slim figure she had when she was in her twenties. Her mom was a beautiful woman on the inside and outside. Everyone seemed to love and respect her. "Hi, Mommy!" She ran over and gave her mom a hug and kiss.

Ms. Maggie hugged her only child. "Hey, baby. I haven't seen you in a long time. What have you been up to?"

Yvette sat down on the chaise that was in the

closet. "Wedding stuff. It's getting really stressful." Ms. Maggie smiled as she browsed through her outfits looking for something to wear.

"Charisse told me you let her go while we were out of town. She was very hurt."

Yvette rolled her eyes. "Look, Ma, I didn't choose her to be my planner, you did. I wanted someone with a good reputation and lots of experience, and Charisse is a new wedding planner. I get supporting black owned businesses and helping each other out, but you don't get married every day. I want the best of everything."

Ms. Maggie shook her head in disapproval-- who did this child really belong to? "Well baby, now you're contradicting yourself. According to Charisse, you had picked out the prettiest Vera Wang gown, and had it altered and paid for it in full. Let me change that-- *we* paid for it, and all of a sudden you didn't want it. According to Charisse, your exact words were, 'you heard about a young up-and-coming African American designer in Richmond. You wanted to help her out and give her some business and exposure.' Is that correct?"

Yvette was caught off guard. "Well, yeah, Ma. I was right. The new gown is amazing, and this is free advertisement for her."

Ms. Maggie still had her back to her daughter. "What I'm trying to figure out is why in the world you would go all the way to Richmond to a plus-size designer when you aren't even close to being plus-sized? Now, don't get me wrong, the young woman is very talented from what I saw when I checked her work, and it's good to give her some exposure, but how did you find out about her?"

Yvette felt herself getting warm. "I went online and searched for African American designers, Ma. Her site came up, and I wanted to see just how talented she was by presenting her with the challenge of designing a wedding gown for a smaller framed woman. She passed with flying colors."

Ms. Maggie decided on her cream-colored pants suit and pulled it out. "What I'm trying to figure out is why didn't you do that before you bought the first gown? And before we left town everything was paid for with the exception of a few small things that Charisse was handling-- I come back to all of these expenses and high credit card bills. Two expensive gowns with accessories, not to mention the $5000 cash advance you took out yesterday on your credit card."

Yvette stood there shocked. "You have been monitoring my spending?"

Ms. Maggie spun around and placed a hand on her hip. "Hell, yeah! Yvette, we give you a generous monthly allowance with the stipulation that you help out with the business and the many foundations we have started. You haven't done any of that. We agreed that you and I would start this mentoring program for these girls and all you have done is plan a party."

Yvette followed her mother into her bedroom. "Ma, that party raised $40,000 for that program."

Her mother sat on her bed and crossed her legs, looking at her spoiled grown daughter. "And you think that's all you need to do? You don't even work with your dad. Hell, I could see if you were down at the office trying to help your future husband out, but all you do is shop, go to parties and take these extravagant trips as if you were the one who worked hard for this money. You don't even bother to come to the meetings or respect us enough to give us a good enough lie as to why you don't show up. Let me tell you something, I don't know where you get this sense of entitlement from, but at 31, you ain't entitled to shit you didn't earn, my child. You grew up watching your father and I try to help our community and give our people the help and resources they need to overcome poverty. Life isn't about shopping and living large. It's about actually living, surviving, and making a difference. Working hard, helping others, sticking together looking out for your brothers and sisters!"

Yvette was annoyed. "Ma, how did we go from me spending money on the most special day of my life to what's going on in the ghetto?"

Ms. Maggie jumped up and got in her face.

"Girl, if you don't wake up and realize what's going on in this world with your people, you just might end up in that ghetto that you love to judge. Your father and I worked hard for what we have. We came from that ghetto, and we never forgot where we came from. That's why we try so hard to provide resources to help those who aren't as fortunate. We try to at least make it safer and easier for them."

Yvette backed away from her mom. "Well, Mommy, you and Daddy's testimony shows that if they really want better, all they have to do is work hard like you guys."

Ms. Maggie looked at her daughter in disbelief-- where did they go wrong? "Yvette, you had better make some changes, and I mean quickly! At the rate you are going, I see life as you know it is about to change drastically. You're about to marry a good man. I think out of respect for your father, he didn't have you sign a prenup. Let me update you on your present financial status-- this month will be the last allowance check you will get from us. The credit cards have been deactivated. Your grown ass is about to be married. That makes you your husband's responsibility. Let me tell you, I've known Charles since he was a teenager. He has grown to be a good man and he deserves a good woman. If you choose not to be that woman he deserves, trust and believe he will find another.

Baby, money is not everything, and I think you're about to find that out."

"I am relieving you of your duties for the mentoring program. You are no longer expected to help at the businesses, not that you ever did anyway. I need for you to find a buyer for that first wedding gown and pay us back the money we paid for it. You also need to pay Charisse her remaining balance."

Yvette was pissed, "You expect me to pay her for doing nothing?"

Ms. Maggie laughed. "And why not? You've been getting paid for doing nothing since you got out of college." Yvette began to cry. It was no use in going to her father because they have always been a unit. She learned that when she was a little girl.

This was the worst! How was she going to get the money for David? Ms. Maggie interrupted her thoughts "Oh, and you can keep the car, but you need to put some insurance on it by the end of the month. We're doing this because we love you, baby. You have to be able to take care of yourself in this world and be more aware of what's going on with our people. You need to learn to have compassion. Charles is a good man. Let him lead you. That is where he came from. And he knows what has to be done. Help him and be his right hand, not some lazy housewife who just wants to spend his money. That's not what he's about. Don't take him for granted."

Yvette stood there in anger. "I can't believe you are doing this to me." And she walked out.

## 24

Tessa was a nervous wreck. She looked over at Sam and wanted him to drive faster but said nothing. Angie called her and told her to hurry to the boutique. There was a fire. What else could possibly go wrong in her life? They could not turn onto the street where her boutique was located. It was blocked off with fire trucks. Tessa jumped out of Sam's truck before he could come to a complete stop and hurried down the street. When she saw all the flames she screamed, Angie was talking with one of the firemen, but she heard her sister's screams. She ran over and hugged her sister and cried with her. Sam walked up and stared at the boutique in disbelief. His heart immediately went out to Tessa. This boutique was her baby.

Tessa stood staring at her dream going up in flames. Was this her punishment for having sex with Sam earlier? "How did you find out, Angie?"

Angie looked but did not speak to Sam. She rubbed her sister's back "I came back to the shop because I left my laptop charger in your office. I pulled up and noticed a light flickering. As I got closer, I realized it was flames. I dialed 911 and thought I could run in and try to save some of the merchandise Tessa, but when I opened the door, the flames were too much! I'm so sorry!"

Angie began to cry. Tessa hugged her sister. "Angie, I'm glad you couldn't go in. I could have lost you too." The two sisters held each other tightly and cried as they watched the firemen put out the fire.

When they finally put out the fire, the fire chief walked over and handed Tessa some papers. He was accompanied by a police officer. "Miss Grant, I think we found the cause of the fire. It seems as if this brick was thrown in the window, along with a container containing gasoline. It looks as if the person broke the window and threw in some gasoline and a match. With all the fabric you had around, it was easy to ignite a fire that would spread throughout the store." After he finished, the officer joined in. "There was another fire just like this one at another store a few weeks ago. We're thinking it's probably some young people with nothing else to do but destroy other people's property. We're in the process of collecting the surveillance tapes from the business of the outside camera view to see if we can find any clues. Here is my card and if you think of anything that may help, please call me."

Tessa thanked both of them. She turned to Sam. "Thanks so much for everything. I'm going to ride with my sister and stay with her tonight. I don't feel like being alone."

Sam gave her a hug. "Tessa, I'm so sorry this is happening to you. Let me know what I can do to help. I can get my crew in here and make everything like brand new for you. No charge. I owe you that much. Just let me know when you want them to get started.

Tessa shook her head. She felt so defeated and weak. "Sam, at this point I'm not so sure when I would want to start over, but I know that I have to. I have responsibilities now." She was talking to Sam, but it was almost as if she was talking to herself.

Sam looked confused. "Tessa, the insurance will take care of all of this. You won't have to pay, I told you I will renovate for free and that will free up your money to replace whatever merchandise was lost.

Tessa looked Sam in his eyes while speaking to her sister-- she knew she had to tell him. "Angie, will you be okay to drive home, and I will meet you there?"

Angie understood. "Yeah, I'm good. I need to get home, Mommy and Daddy are at my house with the kids. Go ahead and handle your business."

Tessa gave her sister a hug, turned around and started walking with Sam back to his truck. He put his arm around her. "Let's go to the park and get some fresh air. We can walk and talk. Do you feel up to it or do you want to go for a drink?"

Tessa moved away from him. She had almost

forgotten about how his fiancé had them followed. "Are you sure this is a good idea?"

Sam put his arm back around her as they continued to his truck. "Look, I'm not concerned about that. My only concern is making sure you're good, Tess." Tessa gave in and they headed to the park. She was feeling anxious, and yet so tired. She just wanted to get this over with.

## 25

Yvette pulled up in front of a small house in Southside Richmond. She had spoken with David and told him they needed to meet, as she didn't want to discuss anything over the phone. She was so pissed at her parents and Charles. She texted him several times and he had not responded. She had no money and she needed to get ahold of some cash quickly for David. She needed to tell David she needed more time, but she was scared he would back out and think she was playing games, even though she had already given him $5000. She knew she would be able to get some cash from Charles, but not that much at one time. She needed to come up with something quickly to convince him to give it to her.

Yvette rubbed her temples and exhaled. She was so stressed, and it was all Charles's fault. She had a good mind to call off the wedding and go to her parents to let them know what their precious Charles had been up to. She wasn't about to give up the lifestyle that Charles could provide for her. She just wanted to ruin Tessa and make her pay for what she had done. She pulled out her phone and called David to let him know she was outside. She had no intentions on getting out of her car in this neighborhood at night. David came out to the porch and motioned for her to come in.

She hesitated but got out of the car and walked quickly towards the small house. Clutching her Gucci purse tightly on her side, Yvette stepped out of her car.

She walked up to David, who, parallel to her, wore nothing but a wife beater and a pair of basketball shorts. He looked so sexy, and you could see the bulge in his shorts. She couldn't help but think of their kiss the other day. "Hey Ma, come in. I have some good news for you." Yvette smiled and followed him into the house. She walked in and saw a guy stretched out on an old couch. She looked at him and smiled, exchanging hellos He nodded his head and kept on watching the 60-inch television. David didn't bother to make any introductions. He told her to follow him down this dark hallway and into this small room.

The room was very warm. There was a fan on the small dresser, but it really didn't help with the heat. There was a queen-sized bed that was unmade taking up the rest of the space in the room. "Sit down and relax, Ma. Nobody is gonna bite you."

Yvette really didn't want to but she didn't want to offend him, so she sat down. "What's the good news?" He smiled and said the job was done. Yvette immediately felt lightheaded and hot. She didn't know if it was from her stressful day, the small room, or what he had just said to her. "What do you mean? I thought you wanted half first?"

David smiled and looked down at her thighs that were exposed by the dress. "Well, I thought about your situation and mine, and decided to give you a break since we were both hurt by the bitch. I went ahead and did it. Just deduct the $5000, and give me the rest and we straight."

Yvette felt her throat go dry and she could barely speak. "What exactly did you do?"

David stood up to turn up the fan. "Let's just say that her staff won't be going into work for a while. Look, I don't want to go into detail. Just know that I did what you asked me to do. Just bring me the rest by the end of the week and we cool".

Yvette began to massage her temples. This headache was getting worse by the minute.

"Look, um David, I'm going to need some more time to come up with the rest. I had a setback and I need to move some things around. I had no idea you were going to act so quickly."

David's eyes went dark, and he just stared at her. "Yo Ma, you came to me and asked me to help yo ass out. You gotta do better than that. A nigga risked his freedom and shit. Don't let me find out you tryna run a game or set a nigga up!" David reached over and grabbed her by the neck.

Yvette placed her hand on his arm trying to

loosen his fingers from around her neck. "David, it's not like that at all, I promise. Just give me a few more days." David looked at her strangely and released his grip from around her neck. He put his hand on her thigh and slowly ran his hand up her dress. Yvette tensed up but she knew better than to move.

"What are you gonna to do to reassure me that you not playing with my money? What you gonna give me right now?" Yvette may not have come from the streets, but she knew what he meant. She opened her thighs and allowed him better access to what he wanted.

David smiled and moved his hand up her dress and pushed her panties to the side and slid his finger inside her wetness. Yvette moaned and opened her legs even wider. David added another finger and began to work them in and out of her pussy. She moaned louder and began to move her hips. All of the sudden, he stopped. She opened her eyes to find out why. He stood up and took off his wife beater and pulled down his shorts. He had no underwear on, and his dick stuck straight out. "Don't just sit there. Take off your clothes."

Yvette got up and began to quickly undress. When she was done, he grabbed her and pushed her down on her knees and stuck his dick in her mouth. She began to gag, but he did not let up. She tried to push him away, but he was too strong. Just when she felt like she was going to throw up, he pulled out of her mouth. She was relieved, but also embarrassed. He grabbed her up from the floor and pushed her back on the bed. He pushed her legs back so far, she thought they would break in two.

Her ankles were on each side of her head. "Hold your legs back and don't move." He commanded. He got on his knees and stuck his two fingers inside her wetness again and began working them in and out really fast.

Yvette began to yell. "Please, don't stop, please!!" He leaned down and began sucking her clit while still moving his fingers. She thought she would lose her mind. He began moaning and sucking her clit harder and it was starting to hurt, but she didn't want him to stop. He got up and leaned over and rammed his dick inside her. She screamed and tried to lower her legs, but he wouldn't let her. He fucked her fast and hard with such intensity, Yvette began to scream. "David, wait! Oh, shit!" She tried to put her hands on his chest to push him back, but he was too strong. She just gave up and continued to moan and scream.

"That's right. Take this dick, bitch."

Yvette began to yell. "I'm coming!" David grunted but he didn't let up, in fact, he went even faster. "You better not come yet. Hold that shit!"

Yvette felt crazy she screamed. "I can't! I just can't!" She began to really scream and shake-- she came so hard she felt like she was going to pass out. David kept right on pumping. She could not catch a break. All she could do was moan and whimper. She felt her body begin to shake again and all she could do was scream.

David finally pulled out of her and straddled her chest. He put his wet sticky dick in her mouth and said "Don't move. Just open your mouth." Yvette did as she was told, as he fucked her mouth. For some reason she began to moan. It was turning her on.

David looked down at her and smiled "Bitch, you like the way that pussy tastes, huh?" He got off of her and commanded her to get on her hands and knees. He spread her cheeks and entered her from behind. Once again, he began to pump fast and hard. She screamed and begged him not to stop. He pumped harder. "You love this dick, don't you? Say you love it!"

"I love this dick! Yes! I love it!"

He pulled out and told her to drop down on her knees he rammed his dick her mouth again and came. "Swallow all that shit and don't you waste any of it." Yvette began to swallow and tried not to gag. He pulled out of her mouth and looked down at her and shook his head. "You bourgeois bitches are the biggest freaks." He laughed and began to get dressed.

She sat on the floor dumbfounded and breathing

hard with his semen all around her mouth. David walked out the room and came back with a wet washcloth and handed it to her. She took it and cleaned herself as best as she could she was sore all over. She put on her clothing and grabbed her purse. It was definitely time to leave. David walked her out. When she got to the living room, the same guy was still on the couch. This time he was looking at her with a smirk on his face. She knew he heard them or was possibly watching. She didn't even bother to say goodbye to him. When they got to her car, David grabbed her arm. She naively thought he wanted to kiss her goodbye.

She stopped and turned around to face him. "You have until Friday, and don't stand me up." Yvette got the message and she got into her car and drove off, feeling sexually satisfied, but even more stressed out. How was that possible?

## 26

Sam walked holding Tessa's hand and it felt like old times. He wished that this night didn't have to come to an end. He wished he could take her hurt and pain away. "Tess, I really don't want you to stress about the boutique. The new one will be bigger and better. Everything happens for a reason, good or bad. Isn't that what you used to tell me?"

Tessa looked at him and smiled. "Let's sit down for a few minutes. I'm really tired." They stopped and sat on a bench still holding hands and looking up at the stars.

Sam felt like he was in heaven with the woman he loved. "Sam, the reason I wanted to see you today wasn't because I needed closure. I really need to tell you something. I'm four months pregnant with your baby. Please don't say anything or try to make me any promises right now. I just wanted you to know. I didn't want to keep it from you, and I know you have a lot going on right now. I just feel like you have a right to know and frankly, at this point, I despise secrets."

"You will be married and starting a new life. I don't want you to think I'm telling you this to stop you from getting married. I know you have a lot going on, but why should I be the only one walking around carrying this? I'm keeping the baby regardless of what you do, but I just wanted you to know. I don't want any drama or confusion in my or the baby's life, so I'm not sure what you're going to do about Yvette if you want to be in this child's life. I refuse to have my child being looked at as a mistake or horrible secret, so you will have to deal with your wife. Take some time to think about this and let it sink in. What happened earlier doesn't change the fact that I don't trust you. But I do trust that you will do the right thing when it comes to your child. It's no longer about us. It's about our child."

Sam sat there stunned. Did she just say that he was going to be a father? He let go of her hand and placed his hand on her stomach. "Oh my God, Tess! Are you sure?"

Tessa placed her hand over his and smiled. "Yes, Sam. I've had an ultrasound and everything. I'm having your baby. I'm still in shock myself."

He looked at her and smirked. "I guess we weren't always careful, huh?"

Tess laughed. "No, we were not." Sam felt happy and had immediate love for this child, and even more for Tessa. He felt like if he took his hand away from her stomach, his child would disappear. This baby was the only living blood relative he had, and he wasn't about to lose it.

After his aunt passed away, he never felt more alone. Sure, the Duncans were there, but there's nothing like blood family. He felt like this baby was a gift from God and a message. He knew exactly what he had to do for the sake of his child. He knew Tessa didn't want him to make any promises to her but nothing nor no one was going to keep him from being a father to his child. He looked up at Tessa and smiled, "Thank you so much for telling me, Tessa." Tessa smiled back at him, and they just sat there together with their hands on her stomach.

## 27

Ms. Maggie sat at the dinner table across from her husband enjoying a delicious turkey wing dinner she had prepared for them. Even though they had a maid, she made sure she cooked for her husband at least twice a week. She never wanted him to get used to another woman's cooking. "This is good, baby. Thanks for cooking for me." She smiled at her husband. He had been saying the same thing to her since the beginning of their marriage 30 years ago.

"Have you heard from our child?"

Ed nodded his head. "As a matter of fact, she called me today and asked me if I had time to go out to lunch with her tomorrow. I asked her why doesn't she just come by the house and eat lunch, so Ethel can cook her favorite crab cakes. She told me she wanted to treat me for a change." Both of them bust out laughing. They knew their daughter very well and they knew she was trying to soften him up to get some money. Ed shook his head. "What I don't understand is why she is trying to get more money. The wedding is paid for, so is the honeymoon. She asked me to have a prenup drawn up for her and I laughed. She said she wanted to protect her inheritance. I assured her that her inheritance is well protected. I love Yvette, but Charlie is doing the right thing controlling the finances! He's worked too hard, and Yvette doesn't work at all. She thinks he is being controlling with his finances, but he is really being wise."

Ms. Maggie agreed with her husband. "Did she mention to you that anything is wrong between the two of them? Charlie has been kind of distant these past few weeks. I know 'Vette can be a lot to deal with, I'm just surprised they made it this far. I would have never thought the two of them could be a match."

Ms. Maggie nodded. "I thought the same thing, but I guess opposites do attract in some cases. Maybe being married to Charlie will bring her back down to Earth. Charlie already told me that he was letting the maid go. He said Vette doesn't work, and he doesn't see any reason why she can't keep the house clean while he's at work."

Ms. Maggie smiled. "Good for him! Yes, Vette is definitely in for a rude awakening."

## 28

Tessa walked up to her sister's door and rang the bell. It was late, but she could tell that her parents were still there. She knew Angie told them she was with Sam tonight and they wanted to know what happened. In spite of everything that happened today, she actually felt a little better and more optimistic about everything. "Girl, I was just about to call you to make sure you were okay." Tessa smiled and walked into her sister's home. She shared a lovely 4-bedroom house in a Chesterfield subdivision with her husband Donte and three girls-- Deja, Dalilah and Dawn.

Her parents sat in the living room eating ice cream. "Hey, Ma. Hey, Daddy."

Mrs. Grant looked up from her bowl. "Don't you 'Hey, Ma' me. We were worried sick about you." She sat down next to her mom and kissed her on the cheek, grabbed her spoon and started eating her ice cream.

"I'm good, Mommy. I'm sure Angie told you I was with Sam. I told him about the baby. I'm giving him some time to let it sink in. We're going to talk in a few days to discuss what's best for the baby. As for the boutique, it's no use in sitting around crying about it. I'm going to rebuild and it's going to be bigger and better!"

George hit the arm of the sofa. "That's what I'm talking about!" He looked at Elizabeth. "That's MY daughter right there!"

Elizabeth looked at him and shook her head. "Tessa, I need for you to be careful when you reopen that shop. Anyone could have gotten hurt, and you need to put up some cameras."

Tessa rubbed her eyes and yawned. She was getting tired. "I will, Mommy. There has been a lot of vandalism in that area anyway. I just need to make my place more secure. It will be fine." She didn't bother to tell them that Sam offered to renovate for her for free. She just didn't have the energy for that conversation.

Yvette didn't make it home from Richmond until after midnight. Charles was already fast asleep. She wanted to go off on him for not answering her calls and not waiting up for her, but right now she needed money from him so it wouldn't be wise to upset him. She undressed and got in the shower-- her body ached all over. She had never had sex like that before. A part of her felt degraded, but then again, she enjoyed it. She was not a fool. She knew David handled her like that for a reason-- she had better figure out how to come up with $20,000.

She got out the shower and began to carefully rub her towel over her sore body. She brushed her teeth and rinsed the taste of David out of her mouth. She had been trying to please Charles every night, but that was definitely not happening tonight. She walked back into the bedroom and slowly got into the bed, careful not to wake up Charles. She was sore, tired, and stressed. She just needed some sleep so she could wake up fresh to figure some things out. Charles lay beside her with his back towards her-- he was relieved that she had not tried to wake him up. He was in for a long emotional day tomorrow and he needed to rest.

Even though her boutique was physically destroyed, Tessa still had work to do. Thank God for modern technology. She still had her info for her orders and all of her other important information in her electronic files. She was now in Angie's home office on her computer making sure the orders were still going to be filled online. She was grateful that the wedding gown was at the dry cleaners being professionally cleaned. She would pick it later, along with her other orders and get them delivered. She put in a call to her insurance company to report what happened-- she was meeting the claims adjuster this afternoon at the boutique so that he could assess the damage.

"Hey, girl, you're up early." Angie walked in and handed her sister a cup of herbal tea.

She had given up coffee until after she had the baby. "Yeah, just trying to get things together, figure out my next steps and come up with a plan. What's on your agenda today?"

Angie sat down across from her sister. "I'm pretty much free. I can pick up the orders from the dry cleaners for you. I will call the clients and let them know what happened, so we can make arrangements to deliver the orders instead of having them pick them up. The good thing is that there weren't any unfinished orders lost in the fire. Everything was finished and had been taken out to be cleaned. God is good, Tessa."

Tessa sighed but agreed. "Yes, he is, Angela. I'm looking at the inventory that was lost along with everything else. I can't even say the amount out loud. I just don't understand why this happened."

Angie nodded. "Tess, stop dwelling on what was lost. You will gain it all back, plus more. We just have a lot of work to do. I'm going to take a shower and get dressed. Mommy is coming over to get the kids. You get ready, I'm taking you home to get dressed. Then, you can tell me what really happened with you and Sam. Don't you think for one minute that I didn't see y'all walking down the street hugged up." Angie got up and walked out. Tessa sat there with her mouth opened in shock.

## 31

Yvette woke up to an empty bed. Charles was already up and she could smell the coffee. She was going to give him a special treat this morning, but she guessed that would have to wait. She eventually made it down to the kitchen. Sam was sitting at the table eating a bagel and drinking a cup of coffee while reading some paperwork. She walked over and poured herself a cup of coffee. "Good morning, babe."

Sam never looked up and mumbled, "Morning." Yvette sighed. Ever since this ordeal with Tessa, he acted as if he hated her. The only time he would show some interest in her was when they made love. Not that he was all that affectionate or talkative before. For the most part, he was easygoing and went along with whatever. It was all different lately, even with money.

He had yet to add her to his bank accounts, or to even discuss finances with her. He still handled all of the household bills. If she wanted to buy anything for the house, she had to go to him for the money or use her funds. He kept an eye on his money and paid attention to everything that went out. It wasn't going to be easy to get him to come

up off of this money for David. "Where is Leticia?"
Yvette noticed the maid was missing.

Charles finally looked up at her. "She is
registering for classes today. She decided to get her
degree."

Yvette was shocked. "What do you mean? And
why didn't she discuss this with me? She just can't
leave us hanging like this!"

Charles just stared at her for a moment. "She
tried to discuss it with you, but every time she asked
for a moment to talk, you were too busy. With what,
I don't know. She stopped me last week and
informed me. I thought it was a great idea."

Yvette shook her head. "So, since you're
handling everything and encouraging the help to
abandon their duties, did you call the agency for
another maid?"

Charles got up to pour himself another cup of
coffee and leaned on the counter to face her. "As a
matter of fact, I didn't. I told Leticia that she could
come here and work around her school schedule.
We don't need a maid anyway-- especially every
day. You're at home all day and we don't have
children. It's really a waste of money. And what
happened to you cooking on some nights? You
haven't cooked a meal since you moved in here with
me, and that was a year ago."

Yvette was trying to stay calm, because she
needed him and wasn't trying to piss him off by

telling him how stupid he sounded right now. "I will cook, but I was thinking of starting a mentoring program on my own eventually and it is going to keep me pretty busy. My parents taught me well, and I'm sure I can do it on my own. Maybe we can start an apprentice program for underprivileged boys. They can come and work for you when they finish school. You can train them on a trade."

Sam was surprised and suspicious at the same time. She had never been interested in helping anyone but herself, "Okay, that sounds interesting. Let me think about it."

Yvette smiled. "Babe, don't wait too long. We need to jump on this. It could be our program with you using your business as a platform to give back to the community. I have so many ideas, and I just want to get started as soon as possible. Maybe I can host a fundraiser, but first we will need to use our cash to get things started." Yvette was amazed at how quickly she came up with that.

Charles looked at her strangely, "That really sounds good, Vette, but right now I have a lot on my plate with other mentoring facilities. Plus, I am working to figure out some other things. What's the story on the teen-mom program you're working on with your mother? Your dad told me you're no longer a part of that?"

Yvette looked at him surprised, how dare her father discuss that with him. "Well, I just felt like it was time for us to make our own name in the community. It's time we stopped being in their shadow." Charles smiled but he didn't say anything. He knew Yvette was full of it.

"Babe, if we're going to do this, I'm going to need access to some cash to fund this project."

Sam smiled. "You are so funny. You think I don't know your parents cut you off? Now you want to milk me. What do you need, 'Vette? Some hair and nails money? Did you see a new bag you just have to get? You and the girls going on a shopping spree?" Yvette cringed inwardly, but she did not react. This conversation was taking a wrong turn. Yvette walked over to Sam and began to rub his dick through his jeans. Charles backed away from her. "You don't have to do that. I'm cool." He walked over to his briefcase and took out his checkbook. "Here's a check for 10 grand, Yvette. Use it wisely. And don't get used to getting this on a regular basis. You need to figure out how to make yourself useful and make your own way. I'm not a bank. I'm not going broke trying to finance your careless spending. I work hard for my money, and I refuse to squander it away. I have a lot going on today, so don't blow up my phone for nonsense."

Yvette took the check and gave him a hug and kiss. She was so glad about the money that she didn't even hear anything he said after 10 grand. "Thank you, baby. And don't worry. I'm about to make you proud that I'm your wife". Charles rolled his eyes, grabbed his briefcase and walked out of the house. He only gave her the money to keep her occupied long enough for him to figure things out and go help Tessa today.

## 32

Tessa and her staff were busy going through the ruins of the boutique to see what they could salvage. She had already met with the insurance adjuster, and he declared the boutique a total loss. She would be getting her check in a few weeks, and now she needed to decide if she wanted to stay at this location or possibly build in another location. "Hey, pretty mama! What do you think you're doing?" She looked up and saw Sam standing there with a carrier of fruit smoothies for everyone. She smiled and walked over to him, careful not to fall. "Seriously, Tessa, I don't think you should be in here. It's too dangerous. Trust me, if you find anything, you're not gonna want to use it."

Tessa wiped the sweat from her brow and looked around, "I know, but it's just so hard to let go." Sam grabbed her hand and helped her walk over the rubble. He led her out of the boutique. He handed her a smoothie and called for the girls to come and get one. Tessa turned to the girls and smiled. "Thanks so much for coming down to help me, y'all. I'm not too sure when I will be reopening but I will keep you guys posted. I know this is your livelihood, and I plan to continue to pay you guys while we're in the process of rebuilding. I'm in the process of trying to figure out a temporary solution until I can reopen." The girls looked pleased at the thought of continuing to get paid. They thanked her and left her alone with Sam.

Someone walked up to her just as the girls were leaving, "Hello. Are you the owner of this store?"

Tessa turned around and faced a woman in her mid-forties. She was standing next to a boy who looked to be about 16. "Yes ma'am, but as you can see, we're not open for business."

The woman looked inside the store through what used to be the window and shook her head in disbelief. The boy looked down at the ground. The woman turned to Tessa, "That's what we came to see you about. My name is Vanessa Carter, and this is my son Calvin. He wants to tell you something." Calvin stood looking down at the ground. Vanessa nudged him.

When he finally looked up, he had tears in his eyes. "Um, me and my friends did this to your store ma'am, and I'm very sorry."

Tessa was stunned and Sam was also. Tessa could feel the tears begin to roll down her face. "But, why?"

Calvin spoke again. "I did it on a dare, well for some Jordans. I know it was stupid and I'm sorry."

Vanessa cleared her throat. "Ma'am, I didn't raise my son to do stupid shit like this. I am a hard-working single mom with five kids and Calvin is the oldest. I try my best to teach good values to my kids and to keep them on the right track." Vanessa looked at Calvin. "When they get around their friends, it's like they lose all common sense! I'm the mama and daddy in my house and Calvin knew if I found out about this, it would be hell to pay. He walked in last night out of breath and smelling like gasoline. I asked him why he smelled like that, and he didn't have an answer for me. Well, I went on my back porch and found an empty gas can. Hell, I don't even own a car. I took my stick and kicked open his room door and got to wailing on his ass until he told me what he did. I made him come down here, so I'm glad you were here. I'm about to take him to the police station because he has to learn that there are consequences for doing stupid shit. I don't know how this will turn out, but I needed him to own up to what he has done. Someone could have gotten killed! Every time I think about it, I get sick." Vanessa began to cry. "The thought of my child doing something like this just for a pair of shoes!"

Tessa looked at the pair and was speechless. She knew she couldn't allow this child to go into the system. That wasn't going to help him. She looked at Sam and she could tell he was thinking the same thing. "Look Ms. Carter, I think we may be able to come up with a solution to help all of us. You don't want your son to get lost in the system. I have a contracting business and we're about to start working on Ms. Grant's shop to get it back up and running. Calvin can come and assist the crew. It's going to be long hours, but it will keep him busy, and he will be learning a trade, as well."

"Calvin what do you want to do when you finish school?" Sam asked. Calvin humped his shoulders and kept looking at the ground. Sam moved and got in his face. "You look at me like a man when I'm talking to you. Don't be shy. You created this. Now you have to be a man and fix it. Do you know you can go to jail for a long time for this? Do you think they're going to care about your tears in jail? Do you think that white man is going to care that you broke your mama's heart and left her alone to take care of your siblings? Do you think they're going to care when those other inmates rape you and beat you down? Do you think Jordan is going to care?"

Calvin looked up at Sam. "No, sir. I know they won't care."

Sam backed up, "Well, good. That's the first step to getting you on the right track. You're the man of your house and you need to start acting like it. Your siblings are looking at everything you do, and you need to give them something positive to look at. Your mom works hard and sacrifices to keep you alive in this world. You need to show her your appreciation by becoming a productive citizen, regardless of your environment and what you're up against. They want you to fail and you have to rise above that. As black men, we have to work harder, be stronger and smarter. So, you don't have room to mess up man!"

Calvin stood taller as Sam spoke and he listened carefully to everything Sam was saying. He never had another man speak to him like that, and it made him really feel bad about what he had done. He turned to Tessa. "I am really sorry for what I have done ma'am, and I will do whatever you want me to do to make this right."

Tessa smiled. "Thank you, Calvin, for being man enough to apologize and confess. And thank you for your willingness to make this right." Tessa gave him a hug and turned around and hugged his mom as well.

"Thank you so much. I don't know how to repay y'all for giving my baby a second chance." Vanessa whispered, as she hugged Tessa back.

Tessa was crying. This baby had her emotions all over the place. "If he was my child, I would want someone to help him if he messed up. I think he is going to be just fine." Vanessa hugged Sam and thanked him also they exchanged contact information to set up a time for Calvin to start. Sam said he would make arrangements for him to be picked up and dropped off. His mom decided to place him on her own house arrest for the rest of the summer. He would go to work and come home. His only outings would be with Sam. Tessa watched them walk away feeling happy, having gained more respect for Sam. Regardless of the circumstances, she was glad he was the father of her child.

## 33

Yvette arrived at David's place in the late afternoon; he was sitting outside waiting for her. She had on a black Victoria Secrets PINK sweat suit and some black and white Nikes. She was in no mood to dress up. She was giving him this ten grand and hopefully he will leave her alone.

Yvette walked up to the house and followed David inside. He stopped in the living room, and she reached in her purse and handed him the money. He took it and sat down to count it. "Is this all of it?" Yvette began to get nervous. "It's ten thousand. That was all I could come up with." David put the money on the worn coffee table and looked at her. "You must think I'm a sucka or something."

Yvette walked up closer to him and began to rub the bulge in the front of his jeans. "Maybe we can work something out for the rest." David smiled, unzipped his jeans and pulled out his hard, long dick. Yvette got down on her knees and took him in her mouth. She began licking and sucking like her life depended on it. David stepped back and pulled her up off the floor. "Take all that shit off!" Yvette undressed quickly. He sat on the couch, and he pulled her down on top of him.

She straddled his lap and he grabbed her head and started kissing her real hard. He began sucking her tongue-- Yvette began to moan as he sucked it harder. He reached down and stuck his fingers inside her. She started to rock her hips back and forth on his fingers. She rose up and moved his hand and grabbed his dick and slid her pussy down on it. She moaned again as she started to ride him. He grabbed her ass and started lifting her up and down on his dick. He took one finger and stuck it in her ass. She squealed and began to bounce up and down on his dick faster. He lifted her up and turned her around. He held her still while he pumped into her fast and hard. She started screaming, "I'm cumming!" She came hard as he pumped harder.

"Oh shit, bitch!" David rammed his dick up into her so hard she could have sworn he moved something inside of her. He held it up in her and she could feel his sperm shooting up inside her. He let go of her and she lifted herself off of him.

He grabbed her head and pushed her down to the floor between his legs and pushed her head down on his dick. "Clean it off." he said gruffly. Yvette knew better than to protest. She licked his dick clean. He pushed her away, sat up, grabbed the money off the table and started counting it. She was going to ask for a cloth to clean up but changed her mind. She grabbed her purse once she was dressed and walked towards the door. "You have one week to get the rest of my money."

Yvette stopped in her tracks. "I thought we just worked that out."

David stopped counting and looked at her smirking. "We did. You gave me some pussy and I gave you more time to get my money." Yvette began to tremble. She wished she had a gun. She would have shot that motherfucker right in his grinning face. She nodded and walked out of the house, to her car and cried all the way back to Norfolk.

## 34

Yvette sat in the den waiting for Angela to arrive with her gown. Apparently, her gown wasn't in the shop during the fire. She was relieved because she really loved that gown. Her body was still sore from the night before, but she couldn't help the feeling of wanting to do it again. The doorbell rang and she immediately got annoyed because she had to answer it herself. She opened the door with a fake smile glued on her face. "Well, hello, Angela. So glad you finally made it. Please come in!" Angela gave a fake smile right back to her and walked in. She wasn't in the mood to make small talk with this chick. It had been a long day, and she was annoyed from the long drive and traffic. "Let me take that from you." Yvette took the gown and hung it on the coat rack. She unzipped the garment bag to inspect it. Once she was satisfied that it was perfect, she zipped it back up. Of course, Angela had a document ready for her to sign, concluding their business.

"So, you said there was a fire?" Yvette asked while signing the document sounding all nonchalant. Angie took the document and examined the check for the remaining balance.

"Yes, some teenagers were being destructive. My sister called me just now to tell me one actually came and confessed to her."

Yvette was stunned. "Confessed?"

Angie looked annoyed and was sorry she even said anything. "Yeah, confessed. He and his friends did it on a dare or something. Look, this concludes our business. Have a nice life." Angie picked up her purse and showed herself out.

Yvette didn't even bother to answer because she was too stuck on the fact that David tried to play her.

## 35

Tessa was exhausted. It had been a long, draining day. All she wanted to do was grab a bite to eat, take a long bath, and curl up in her own bed. Between the baby and all of the drama, she just wanted to relax. Just as she was about to step in the tub her phone rang. It was Sam. "Hey, Sam. Is everything okay?" Tess asked nervously.

"Yes, I just wanted to make sure you made it home and that you're okay. You had quite a day today"

Tessa stepped into the tub. "I'm fine. Just really tired. I'm in the bathtub now. I forgot that I have a doctor's appointment tomorrow. I need to get some rest because it's an early appointment. You're welcome to join me."

Sam perked up. "In the tub?"

Tessa laughed. "To the doctor's appointment. You can listen to the baby's heartbeat. It's too early to know the sex. I think I want it to be a surprise."

Sam was overjoyed at the invitation. "Of course, I will be there, and to every appointment from now on. Tess, thanks so much for including me!"

"You sound so excited." Tessa giggled. "My appointment is at 8am. I will text you the address.

Now let me finish my bath and go to bed. And thanks for everything today. That was a great thing you did!"

Sam laughed. "That was a great thing WE did Tessa. We think alike. We make a good team."

Tessa didn't respond to that statement. "You have a good night, and I will see you in the morning." She hung up the phone feeling happy and confused.

## 36

Charles hung the phone up full of emotions. There was no way he could marry Yvette when his heart belonged to his baby and Tessa. He was lecturing this kid about consequences, being a man and responsibility, yet he wasn't practicing what he preached. He needed to make this right, regardless of the consequences. He loved Ed and Ms. Maggie, but he had to do what was best for his child. He called Ed and asked if he could stop by to speak with him and his wife. He wanted to tell them what was going on before their daughter put her evil spin on things.

Charles walked into the Duncan's den and his stomach was doing somersaults. They both were sitting on the sofa sipping their drinks. "Charlie, come on in and fix yourself a drink." Ed motioned for him to help himself. Sam wasn't a guest. This was his home. Sam made himself a scotch on the rocks and sat in the loveseat across from the only parents he had known for the past 20 years. The thought that it might be coming to an end made him sad. Ms. Maggie smiled at Charles. "So, what did you want to talk about? Is everything okay? What is that child of ours up to these days?"

Charles took a long sip of his scotch. It burned going down and warmed his insides. "I needed to tell you some things that have happened, because I have made some decisions. I wanted to talk to you guys, face-to-face, to explain everything myself. You might not want anything to do with me after I say what I have to say. Even though that's not what I want, but I'm prepared to accept it."

Ed sat straight up and grabbed his wife's hand. "What is it, Charlie? I can't imagine anything being that bad."

Ms. Maggie shushed her husband. "Charlie, you have us worried. Tell us what is going on."

Charles cleared his throat and began to speak. "Let me just say that I am very thankful for the both of you. I know that I wouldn't be where I am in my life if it wasn't for you all. You all are the only family I've had for the past 20 years. You treated me like I was your son, and I love you all so much for that."

Charles continued. "When Yvette and I started hanging out, I didn't really think anything of it. I was so focused on working and getting my business started, that I hadn't put much thought into what was going on with us. That is, until she brought it to my attention that we were a couple, and how happy you guys were that we had finally gotten together. I didn't know what to say. I just decided not to do anything about it because I didn't want to disappoint you guys or embarrass your daughter. I just went along with the relationship because everyone was so happy about it. I felt like I couldn't express my true feelings and risk you all looking at me differently."

The Duncans watched Charles and listened intently as Charles continued. "I thought that I would lose the only family I had. I know that was very selfish of me. Almost three years ago, I went to Richmond to renovate this space for a boutique. I met the owner to give her an estimate, and we hit it off. I found her pleasant to talk to. She was funny, smart, down to earth and not to mention beautiful. I found myself finding reasons to show up to her shop. I actually started working on her shop myself and got an apartment in Richmond, so I wouldn't have to drive back and forth every day. Yvette never questioned it because she was never interested in my actual work details. She was only interested in the money. As long as I funded her expensive girl's trips and showed up for those parties, she couldn't care less about me spending long hours working on this big project in Richmond."

"I was able to drum up more business in Richmond and it made sense to spend at least 3 days out of the week there expanding the business. Before I realized it, me and Tessa were actually dating, and we fell in love with each other." Ms. Maggie and Ed looked at each other at the mention of Tessa's name. Sam continued, "I came home one day and imagine my surprise when Tessa was sitting in my living room going over wedding dress designs with Yvette."

Ed mumbled "Oh, shit."

Sam looked at Ed. "Yeah, that's what I said. Apparently, your daughter hired a PI and had me followed. She went to Tessa's boutique and convinced her to design a wedding gown for her. Now let me say this, Tessa is a very beautiful plus-size woman, and she specializes in designing clothing for plus-size women. Apparently, Yvette offered her a large amount of money with the promise of exposure, because the wedding would be the event of the year. She also mentioned that she and her family were very well known and like to give back to the community by supporting new black owned businesses. Tessa agreed and signed a contract to do the gown. Yvette planned for both of us to be at the house where she called herself busting us and proceeded to degrade Tessa. She held her to the contract to finish the gown or else she and her family would ruin her and have her blackballed. She also threatened to expose me to you guys for being the cheating son of the bitch that I am."

"I had to stay away from Tessa or else she was going to expose me, and you would blackball me. I tried to obey her wishes, and I did until Tessa informed me that she is pregnant with my child. It's amazing how a child can make you step up to the plate and man up in situations. I'm saying all of this because I can no longer be with your daughter. I know this is fucked up and I should have said something sooner. I'm willing to own up to the part I played in this mess, and I understand if you want nothing else to do with me. I realize you guys have spent a lot of money on this wedding and I promise to pay you back. The truth is, I love you guys very much, but I am not in love with your daughter. I have been a selfish coward for cheating on her and letting it go this far."

"I can't change what has happened, but I can try to make things right. I have a responsibility to my child to make sure that I am someone he or she can trust and look up to. I need to be there for my child and marrying a woman I don't love will only add to the other dishonorable things I have done. I need to put a stop to it."

Ed and Maggie sat and stared in disbelief. Ed spoke first. "Charlie, I must say I am disappointed in you for several reasons and some of them are not the reasons you think. I'm disappointed that you didn't trust that Maggie and I loved you enough to want you to be happy. If you didn't love our daughter, all you had to do was say so. Our relationship with you wasn't based on you marrying our daughter. We were shocked when she told us y'all were marrying. We knew she wasn't your type, but we left that for you all to figure out.

"I am also disappointed in how you handled everything. I taught you to be an honorable man, Charlie, and I always told you all a man had was his word and honor. You running around cheating wasn't fair to Yvette or Tessa. I'm not disowning you, because you are family, and you always will be family. You need to make this right. It's not going to be easy especially when you face Vette. But it's the right thing to do and she will survive. I'm not defending her actions, but I guess she was hurt. That's not a reason to try to control and manipulate people, especially using our name, but that's a conversation we will have with her."

"We still love you, boy, and you need to do right by Tessa and take care of your child. I guess I understand how you feel because I was young and made a mess out of some things myself. I'm still trying to make peace with certain things. But, son, regardless of what happens with you and Tessa, you make sure you stay in that baby's life because you will live to regret it if you don't. One more thing, we will be sending you an invoice for this wedding, I want my money!"

Charles felt like a weight had been lifted off of him. He got up, walked over to Ed, and the two men shared an embrace. Ms. Maggie got up and hugged him also and told him she loved him. She didn't have anything to add to what her husband said. She was busy thinking on this other issue. Like she always said, *'What's done in the dark always comes to the light.'*

Ed looked at his wife when Sam left and shook his head. "Maggie, shit is about to hit the fan."

Maggie felt chills go through her body. "Eddie, baby, we need to call George and Elizabeth and find out how much they know."

Ed got up to pour himself another drink. "They don't know anything. They would have called us by now."

Maggie took a sip of her wine and closed her eyes trying to digest everything that was going on and what was about to happen.

"Eddie I'm going to give them a call first thing in the morning".

Yvette picked up her phone and dialed David. "Hey Ma, tell me something good." David sounded excited. Yvette was furious.

"You lied to me! You didn't do a fucking thing but take my fucking money! I'm not giving you another dime!"

David laughed. "Calm down, baby. No need to get upset. Now stop all that cursing and get yo hot ass down here and bring me the rest of my money. Maybe, I will bless you with some more of this dick that you love."

Yvette was so mad she began pacing back and forth. "Nigga, I'm not giving you another dime!" She disconnected the call and screamed. She couldn't believe that ghetto thug played her. This is the very reason why she didn't understand why her parents tried to help them. They were just no good.

Her phone went off and she saw the message from David. She opened it and saw it was a video. When, it began to play she nearly shit on herself. She was in the video bent over yelling how she loved his dick. The next one was her on her knees with his dick in her mouth and cum running down her face. Her phone rang, and it made her jump.

It was David.

"I think you better get yo ass to Richmond and bring me my money. I don't think Daddy and Mommy Duncan would appreciate seeing their baby acting like a porn star, neither would your fiancé. Yeah, you didn't tell me who your daddy was. you lucky I don't snap your neck for lying to me."

Yvette could barely speak. "I didn't lie to you."

David laughed. "You still lying. Tessa didn't have your man arrested. As a matter of fact, they showed up at the boutique the night of the fire together. Yeah, I keep my ears to the street. You thought you were smarter than a nigga. You tried to play me, and you got played. I went up to the boutique that night to see how everything was set up and make plans, but those lil niggas beat me to it. Then, just as I was about to leave, guess who comes running down the street? Your fiancé and Tessa. That's when I decided to check some things out for myself, because the way they were acting together didn't match that bullshit story you fed me."

David laughed into the phone. "But it's all good, Ma. I'mma give you a pass this time, as long as you give me my money. I would hate to see what happens if your people really see how you give back to us poor folks in the hood." He laughed again. He suddenly stopped laughing and began to talk real low into the phone. "You better bring me my money or else. You got until the end of the week." He disconnected the call. Yvette sat on the side of the bed and started to cry.

## 38

Elizabeth had a strange look on her face when she hung up the phone. "Lizzie, who was that on the phone? What's wrong, honey?" George Grant sat and waited for his wife to respond.

"That was Margaret on the phone." George felt his heart skip a beat.

"What did she want?"

Elizabeth sat next to her husband and held his hand.

"She said the young lady Sam is engaged to is their daughter, Yvette, and Sam is about to break off the engagement, because he doesn't love her. He loves Tessa." George stood up and walked over to the window and looked out at the children riding their bikes up and down the street.

He thought back to the day he taught Tessa how to ride her bike without training wheels. She made him promise not to let go of her before she started to peddle. He could see the fear all over her cute little chubby face. When she started to peddle, he didn't want to let go because he promised her he wouldn't, but he knew he had to. She rode that bike all the way to the end of the street before she realized she was riding on her own. She was so excited, she jumped off the bike, left it, and ran back and jumped in his arms. *"Daddy, Daddy I did it! I rode it by myself, and I didn't fall!"* She was so proud of herself, and so was he. Then she stopped and looked at him curiously. *"Daddy, you promised not to let me go and you did. What if I would have fallen?"* George looked at his little girl and kissed her on her cheek. *"Daddy knew you could do it. That's why I let go. And it you had fallen, Daddy would have been there to pick you up. I will always be here to pick you up if you fall."*

George's eyes began to water thinking about that memory. He turned around and looked at his wife. "Our family has been through enough Lizzie, especially Tessa. In her condition, she-"

"Yes, she has been through a lot because of secrets and lies, but she is strong. It's time to tell the truth. This has gone on too long. I've been thinking and praying about this every day since she was born. George, that's a long time to carry something. She needs to know the truth and soon."

George nodded his head and walked toward the door. "I need to take a walk to clear my head." Elizabeth didn't say anything to her husband, because she understood how he was feeling.

She picked up the phone and called Margaret Duncan back. "Hey, this evening at six will be fine. Everyone will be here for dinner." Elizabeth hung up the phone and said a prayer. She prayed for guidance and understanding that evening.

## 39

Tessa pulled up to the doctor's office and immediately spotted Sam standing in front of the building-- he was waiting for her. He looked so handsome in his jeans and polo shirt. She could still see his muscular build through his shirt.

He walked over to her car and opened her door. She smiled and stepped out of the car. She was wearing a blue-and-white print maxi dress she designed. With her growing belly, a maxi dress and flip-flops were the easiest things to wear. Her hair was styled in micro braids and pulled up into a bun.

"Good morning, beautiful."

Tessa smiled at him. "Good morning to you." They walked into the building and into the waiting room. Before they could sit down, the nurse recognized Tessa and called them to the back.

Once Tessa was prepped for the sonogram, the doctor started the examination. The thumping sound of their baby's heartbeat filled the room. She looked at Sam and saw tears rolling down his face. He couldn't take his eyes off the monitor. The doctor pointed out the baby's body parts before printing the sonogram pictures.

Sam kept staring at them all the way to the car.

He went to hand them to Tessa, and she held up her hand. "Those are yours to keep. I have many."

He smiled from ear to ear, pure joy radiated off of him. "Thanks, Tess. I still can't believe I'm going to be a father." He hugged her and kissed her on the lips. He opened her car door for her to get in. He leaned over and stuck his hand in the car and placed his hand on her belly. "I would take you out to lunch, but I have an important appointment. So, would you like to go to dinner with me? I need to discuss some things with you."

Tessa wondered what he wanted to discuss. "I can't do dinner; you know we have dinner once a week at my parent's house. I'm going to have to take a rain check."

Sam backed up looking disappointed. "Oh, okay. How about tomorrow? I can bring breakfast over to your place." Tessa agreed to breakfast, and they said their goodbyes. She was tired, and she was going home to catch a nap before going to her parent's house.

## 40

Yvette sat on her and Charles's bed wearing nothing but a thong. Charles texted her this morning saying he wanted to see her at the house this afternoon. She needed to give him some good lovin' so he would come up off some more of his money.

She thought about David, and she felt disgusted. She knew she needed to get this crazy thug his money and stay away from him. He had enough information to ruin her life, and she wasn't having that. She heard Charles walk in and call her name.

"I'm up here, babe." She laid back and spread her legs.

Charles walked in and looked at her lying on the bed with her legs open. He looked away and told her to come down to the kitchen. He walked out of the bedroom and down the stairs and waited for her in the kitchen.

Yvette was confused. She got up and put on her robe and hurried down to the kitchen. "What's going on with you?"

Charles was leaning on the counter looking down at the floor. The sound of her voice made him look up at her. "Have a seat, Yvette."

She sat down and he sat across from her. He

reached in his pocket and handed her a check. She took the check, and her eyes got big, "Charles this is a check for $25,000! Is this for the apprentice program?"

Charles looked sad and shook his head. "Yvette, I can't marry you. I'm not in love with you, and I never have been."

Yvette began to panic. "Charles, whatever is going on, we can fix it. We can fix this. I will start helping you more with the business, and when this foundation is up and running, we will be a power couple. Just give it a chance. I know we both did things to each other, but I forgive you, don't you forgive me?"

Charles looked at her and grabbed her hands. "Yvette, you deserve to be with someone who is in love with you, and that's not me. I was wrong for letting things get this far out of control. I have to man up and start being honest. I'm not the man for you, Yvette, and I apologize for leading you on or making you believe that we can have a life together. I know your parents cut you off. That's why I'm giving you the money so you can take care of yourself until you find a job or something. I'm putting the house up for sale and you can stay until the house is sold. I will get myself a townhouse or condo. This house is too big for one person."

Yvette began to cry. "You're going back to her, aren't you?"

Charles thought for a moment, carefully thinking over each word. "It's not about Tessa. I shouldn't have gotten engaged. I wasn't in love with you, Yvette. I don't mean to sound cruel, but at this point, I don't know how else to get through to you."

He stood up and walked to the refrigerator for a bottle of water and leaned against the counter while drinking it. Yvette stood up and began pacing back and forth. She was pissed. "I hope you don't think you can just throw me a check and get off scot-free, motherfucker. My Daddy made you! You would be in the ghetto, in jail, or dead if it wasn't for him! And this is how you treat his daughter? I hope that fat bitch is worth you losing everything, because when my father finds out how you treated me, you will be back in the ghetto where you belong!"

Charles shook his head. "Yvette, I talked to your parents yesterday and told them everything. Everything. Meaning my part and your part. They know everything."

Yvette ran across the kitchen and slapped him so hard he spit water out of his mouth. He looked at her like she was crazy. "How dare you go to MY parents and discuss my business. You're nothing but a coward, Charles! A nobody! A wannabe! I tried to mold you into a real man, but you're just a pussy and ghetto ass punk. Take your sorry ass back to that fat bitch. After a while, she's not even going to want your sorry ass! I can't believe you went crying to my parents!"

Charles laughed to keep from putting his hands on her. "I'm going to pack up some things and leave tonight, because I see we're not going to be able to stay in here together. Like I said, take that money as a token of my apology and get the fuck out of my life. You can stay here until the house is sold. After that, I don't give a fuck where you go."

Yvette got back in his face and pointed her finger at his nose. "Oh, now the real 'Charles', 'Sam', or whoever the fuck you are is coming out!"

Charles put his face real close to hers. "You asked for him, and bitch you got him. You let that be the last time you put your fucking hands on me." He gave her a death stare that made her back up. Charles walked past her and walked up to the bedroom to pack. Yvette looked at the check on the table, got down on her knees and began to cry. She felt like her world was crumbling all around her. As much as she wanted to rip up this check and throw it back in his face, she knew that she couldn't. She had to figure out how to make him pay. This time, he wouldn't recover from it.

## 41

Tessa arrived a little late to her parent's house. She just could not get out of her bed. She called her mom to try to get out of going over there, but her mom wouldn't hear of it. When she pulled up, she noticed an unfamiliar Mercedes parked in front of her parent's house. She got out and rang the bell. Her father answered the door with a weird smile on his face. "Hey, Daddy!" He grabbed her and hugged her tightly. "Daddy, I can't breathe."

He let her go. "Sorry, baby, I'm just so glad to see you."

She laughed and kissed him on the cheek. "I missed you, too, daddy, and you can hug me as tight as you want."

She walked in the living room and a familiar looking older couple was sitting on the couch. Tessa smiled and spoke to them. Her mother walked into the living room and introduced her to the couple. "Tessa, this is Edward and Margaret-- Edward and Margaret, this is our Tessa."

The couple got up and shook her hand. Margaret smiled at her. "Your mother tells me you're expecting! Congratulations!"

Tessa smiled back. "Thank you."

Her husband smiled and said "Yes, congratulations! You look radiant!" Tessa blushed and said another *thank you*. She kept looking at them, they looked so familiar.

"So how do you know my parents?"

Elizabeth rushed into the living room, "Tessa, baby, come on in here and eat. I made a plate for you."

Tessa didn't get up. "I'm not hungry right now, Mommy. Can you wrap it up for me?"

Her mother looked nervous. She walked over to the stairs and yelled for her other daughter. "Angie, come down and join us in the living room so we can have a little chat."

Tessa looked at her parents. They were acting really weird.

Angie came down the stairs. She was upstairs putting on a movie for the kids to watch while the adults had this important meeting her parents had suddenly called. "I see you finally dragged yourself out of the bed." Tessa hugged her sister, where she quickly whispered in her ear. "Do you know what this is all about?"

Angie whispered back. "I have no idea. Mommy just kept insisting that you come over and she made me stay until you got here. Who are these friends we have never heard of?" Tess humped her shoulders and sat down next to her sister on the love seat.

She looked at her parents, and Edward and Margaret sitting across from them looking uncomfortable. Her mom finally cleared her throat and spoke. "I know you girls are wondering why we are all here today and why Edward and Margaret joined us at our family dinner. I'm about to tell you girls something that I probably should have revealed to you a long time ago. I want you to understand that we love you both very much, and every decision we made at the time was what we all thought was best. We only wanted to do the right thing. Now, thinking back, it looks as if we should have handled things a lot differently. We can't change the past, and what's done is done. The only thing we can do now is try to make sure we do the right thing going forward."

Tessa was even more confused, as was Angie., "Mommy, what are you talking about?"

Elizabeth looked at her oldest daughter with a sad look. "Tess, please don't interrupt. I'm trying to explain to you now. Just give me a chance to get it all out before you ask questions. This is very hard for me." Angie squeezed her sister's hand. This was making her nervous. Tessa just sat and remained silent. Elizabeth continued "Ed, Margaret, your daddy and I went to the same college. Ed and I were best friends at one time. We went to high school together and lived in the same housing projects. He was a year older than me and we always hung out in the same circles. We ended up going to the same college and remained friends. I met your daddy my second year of college and we had this on-again-off again relationship."

"Your daddy was what you guys call *'a player'* in college, and that had a big impact on our relationship. One night, your daddy and I had a big argument. It was the biggest one we ever had. We both knew it was over. I was so upset, so to cheer myself up, I went with my girlfriends to a party. My girlfriends ended up leaving me to go off with their boyfriends and I was left to try to get back to my dorm by myself. I ran into Ed at the party, and he drove me back to my room. I was a crying mess, and I didn't want to be alone. Ed came back up to my room with me and we talked, and I cried for hours."

"I guess we both let our hormones get the best of us and ended up going too far. I didn't realize I was pregnant until, I was almost 4 months, because I was stressed with my grades and your grandmother had taken a turn for the worse with her cancer-- I was going back and forth home while trying to maintain my grades at school. By then, Ed and I continued with our friendship and never spoke again about what happened. One day, the doctor called the family up to the hospital because there was nothing more they could do for your grandmother. She was on her way to glory. I was holding her hand when she took her last breath. I will never forget that. I cried and kissed her cheek and the next thing you know I was laying on the hospital bed myself with your grandfather and uncles standing over me."

"I found out I was pregnant the very same day my mama left me. I was so confused and distraught. My mama was gone, I was having a baby, and I wasn't even finished with school or married. How was I going to take care of a baby alone? Your grandfather, bless his heart, told me that the baby was a blessing to replace my mama. I really believed that, and I still do. My daddy looked at me and asked, *'Do you think George will be happy?'*"

"That's when it dawned on me-- this was not George's baby. I hadn't been with George in that way in over six-months. He was running around with other women too much. I looked at my daddy and began to cry. I spilled it all to my daddy, because my mama was gone, and he was all I had left in this world. He insisted that Ed step up to the plate, but Ed was already engaged to Margaret. We weren't in love and were never in a relationship. We were just friends that made a mistake and crossed the line. George heard about my mama and called me. He stayed with me every day and was a comfort to me through the whole process dealing with the loss of my mama."

"He made himself available to me day and

night. He wanted to prove to me that he had changed. On the night of my mama's funeral, I told him what happened between Ed and me-- and that night, I confessed to him that I was having Ed's baby. I expected him to leave me then and there. He wanted to know what I was going to do. He knew Ed and knew he was engaged to Margaret. I told him I hadn't told Ed about the baby; he told me I needed to, and he asked if he could be there when I did. I agreed because I was scared to death. We met that next day with Ed. I told Ed that I was pregnant by him. He was really shocked and didn't have much to say at the moment. I think George's presence intimidated him and he felt uncomfortable. I told him I knew he was about to marry Margaret, and I didn't expect him to be a father to my baby because I didn't want to interfere with his happiness. I just felt he had a right to know."

"Ed said he wanted to take care of his responsibility, and he just needed to talk to Margaret, because he really loved her, and he didn't want to hurt her. At that moment George spoke up. He told Ed that if it was okay with him, he would like to raise the baby as if it was his. He told him he was planning on asking me to marry him after my mama's funeral and he would take care of us. He told Ed he wasn't trying to take his baby away from him, but it would be better for the baby to grow up being and feeling loved with both parents in the same house. No one would have to know the difference. He knew he had been acting like a fool and he needed to show me that he really loved me and anything that was connected to me. I was shocked, as was Ed. After some time and several discussions, we decided that Ed and Margaret were going to marry, and George and I would marry expecting a baby."

"A few months later, I had the most beautiful baby girl, and Ed only asked one thing. He asked if I could name her Tessa, after his mother that was murdered by her drug addicted boyfriend. We all agreed. Ed and Margaret sent money faithfully every month for you Tessa, that's why you had such a large college fund. We took every penny and saved it for your college education."

Tessa was in shock. She couldn't speak. Angie put her arm around her sister in support. "So, you're saying that Daddy is not Tessa's daddy, and this man is?"

Elizabeth looked down at her hands. "Yes, that's exactly what I'm saying. I wanted to say something for so long, but when Ed became a congressman and moved into the public eye, I just didn't want to cause a scandal for him or subject Tessa to it either. You have to know this was hard for all of us, for different reasons. We wanted you to be happy, Tess, and we also wanted to protect you. In our minds, it was just never a right time to tell you."

Tessa finally spoke and looked at Ed as if she was just seeing him for the first time. "You're Ed Duncan, the congressman from Tidewater?"

Ed finally spoke, "Yes, Tessa and I want you to know, like your mother said. We all just wanted to do what was best for you. It was a different time back then. We were all just trying to survive in those times. The situation was just so, so-"

"Embarrassing? Inconvenient? Messy? Which adjective are you looking for, Congressman? And Mommy and Daddy, how could you go so long without telling me who my real father was?"

George stood up and went over to comfort his daughter. "Tessa, I am your daddy in every way except for biologically. I love you just like I love Angie. Have I ever made you feel like I loved you any less?"

Tessa jumped away from his embrace. 'That's not the point-- don't try to deflect. The point is, that all of you lied to me. I would never do that to my child!" Just as the words came out of her mouth, she realized something else. "You mean to tell me that Yvette Duncan is my half-sister? You mean to tell me the bitch is related to me? Now I see why we are all having this come-to-Jesus moment right now. All the skeletons are about to fall out of the closet because of what went down with me and her."

"Now all of a sudden, it's the right thing for me to know that I have a half-sister that probably wants me dead because I was sleeping with her fiancé. Y'all want to come clean now because I'm having a baby with my half-sister's fiancé. More scandal in this family and the Duncans get to maintain a perfect image." Tessa was so angry that she couldn't even cry. She looked at Angie. "Can you believe this shit, Angie? They lied all of these years?"

Angie didn't know what to say. This was all getting too real for her. She got up and just put her arms around her sister to try to calm her down. "Tess, you have to calm down. Remember the baby. That's what is important right now, the baby is." Tessa pulled away from her sister, feeling like the love and emotion of her hug was going to make her cry and she did not want to cry. She was tired of crying.

"A child is supposed to trust their parents and to tell the truth, I have learned something from this. I will never lie to my child, and my child will grow up knowing exactly who he or she is. Even if their father is married to someone else. Is that why y'all told me this? Was the situation a little familiar to y'all? What's with you people and secrets? And Margaret, did your daughter tell you how she treated me? Even though I didn't know about Sam and her? Did you people raise her to be like that? Is that what money and privilege does to you? Maybe I should be happy I didn't grow up with you in my life. I damn sure didn't want to turn out like her crazy ass!"

Elizabeth had heard enough. "Tessa, I know you're upset but you're not gonna sit here and be disrespectful to us! I'm still your mama!"

Margaret stood up and walked over to Tessa and smiled gently at her. "Elizabeth, I understand her pain. Tessa, I want you to know that we didn't raise Yvette to be the way she is. I just recently found out about what happened when Charlie told us." Tessa looked at her-- like, who the hell is Charlie? She forgot about his other name. Margaret smiled again. "When Charlie came and told us everything. I already knew about you making a gown for her and I was confused because she already had a gown. I knew she was up to something, but I hadn't quite put two-and-two together. Tessa, if we knew she was treating you, or anyone else, like that, we would have nipped it in the bud. Yvette is very entitled and selfish, and we are still trying to figure out where we went wrong with her."

"I want you to know that Ed has been watching your every move since you were born. That was the hardest decision he had to make 35 years ago. I myself wasn't sure if it was the right thing, but like George said, we did the best we could during those times. Your parents have been so generous by keeping us posted on all of your accomplishments and even your setbacks. We are equally proud of the woman you've become. Everyone was so young and still trying to figure out who they were during that time. It just all made sense at the time. We all knew this day would come; we just couldn't predict what the circumstances would be. Every night, Ed would look on your website and send it to his friends to try to get your name out there to try to generate business for you. He has driven by your boutique so many times just to look in and was always excited coming back telling me how many customers were in there. I myself have sent some friends to you. You are very talented."

Ed got up and joined his wife. "Tessa, please don't be mad at us. We all love you very much. We made these decisions out of love for you. I have been following your life all along. I wanted to do so much for you, but I knew I was limited because of the situation. George is a good man, maybe a better man than me. I don't know if I, or any other man, could have done what he did. He loves you to death. You are his daughter just as much as you are mine, if not more. You and he have a bond that we will never have. I know this is a lot to take in, but I would like to have a relationship with you and for us to get to know each other better. I would also love to be a part of my first grandchild's life. We are all truly sorry if we did not handle this the right way, but we just didn't know what the right way was. Even now, I'm not so sure of what the right way would have been. Your mama and I were friends. So, I didn't want to leave her alone raising my baby, but at the same time, I was in love with Maggie and your mama was in love with George. If we would have gotten together, it would have been a disaster, and you wouldn't have grown up in a house of love."

"If I thought for one minute that George wasn't treating you right, I would have exercised my rights and got you out of here. You had a great life Tessa, and I know this all feels like a betrayal to you but that really wasn't our intentions. We did all of this out of love for you."

Tessa stood up. She felt so tired. "I think I've heard enough. I don't want to say anything else or be disrespectful, but I have to go. I need time to myself to think. Thank you all for coming clean, I'm sure you all will sleep better tonight."

Tessa got up and her sister followed her out to her car. "Tessa, I am speechless, I just don't know what to say."

Tessa hugged her sister and got into her car. "Angie, this is what happens when you keep secrets. I have always despised secrets. Do me a favor and always be honest with my nieces. This is a cruel world, and they have to at least be able to trust that their parents will always be up front with them."

Angie leaned over and kissed her sister on the cheek. "Tess, try to go home and get some rest. Call me if you want to talk some more. Text me to let me know when you get home safely. I'm going in here to gather my girls and head home. I think I have heard enough for the day myself." Tessa drove off feeling numb. She thought about calling Sam, but she remembered that he somehow played a part in this mess and decided against it. She just wanted to go home and sleep and hope she would wake up tomorrow to find out that this had all been a bad dream.

## 42

Elizabeth sat on her couch and cried, but she was crying because she felt as if a weight had been lifted off her. A weight that had been on her for 35 years. She knew that Tessa was hurt and confused, but given some time, she knew she would come around. Tessa knew that she was loved, and that's all that really mattered in the end. George sat by his wife and hugged her. "Baby, we did the right thing and it's over now. Tessa will come around."

Elizabeth laid her head on her husband's chest. "I know, honey. We knew this day would come. Tessa is strong and very smart. She will be just fine."

Ed and Margaret sat on the loveseat and held hands. They still had work to do. They needed to talk to Yvette and deal with her issues, but also tell her about her sister. "George and Elizabeth, I think we have done enough today. We're going to hit the road. I hope Tessa will be okay and will accept my request to be a part of her and the baby's lives. I feel like I missed out on so much, and I just want to be a part of this chapter in her life." George stood and shook Ed's hand. "I'm sure after giving it some thought, she will realize she wants the same thing.

Tessa is a smart girl with a good heart."

Elizabeth rose and hugged Ed and Margaret. The four of them walked outside to the Duncans' car. They said their goodbyes and the Duncans headed home.

## 43

Yvette found herself in Richmond yet, again-- this was the last time, as far as she was concerned, and after depositing the check from Charles she took out the cash for David. She had some decisions to make about her life. She got a call from her parents this morning asking her to come over later. She figured since Charles spilled the beans about what was going on between them, they wanted to talk to her and get her side of the story. She needed to come up with something fast to keep them on her side so they'd feel bad enough to help her out again. Her phone went off-- looking at the name, she quickly picked up. "I am pulling up to the house now, David." He hung up the phone without saying anything.

She shook her head and clenched her jaw; she would be glad when this was over. She got out of the car and looked around. The block seemed to always be quiet, considering the area. The sun was shining, and it was very hot-- she decided to wear a pair of cutoff jeans, a tank top, and flip flops. These days she was not in the mood to dress up. All this drama was really stressing her out and she barely had an appetite lately. Every time she turned around there was bad news, and she didn't know how much more she could take. She needed to get back in with her parents, and fast-- this life of struggling was not for her.

David swung open the door before she could even walk up on the porch. He looked at her attire and smiled. "I see we really slumming today, huh?" Yvette ignored his comment, instead she walked in and sat on the couch. She no longer had reservations about being in the house, considering all that had taken place the last few times she was there.

David walked over to her and bent over and kissed her. She leaned up and kissed him back. She told herself this was the last time she would be doing this. He stood her up and pulled down her jeans. She reached down and pulled down his basketball shorts and he lifted her up in the air. She wrapped her legs around him and began to moan while grinding her pussy onto his dick. She reached down and grabbed it, positioned it at her entrance. She slowly slid down his length and moved up and down on it. David grunted and helped her move up and down on his dick. She began to moan and hug around his neck tightly. He pulled her all the way down on his dick and she screamed out. She felt a sharp pain and tried to move back some, but he held her tightly. "David, it's hurting!" David eased up and let her down.

He bent her over the couch and roughly entered

her from behind. He pumped her hard and fast. She was struggling to keep up. She was sore and in pain, but for some reason she came so hard that it scared her, and she cried out. He grunted and pushed his dick all the way inside her until it could not go any further. He held it there. He grunted and began to move from side to side grinding it deeper inside of her. She felt him shoot his sperm deep inside of her. "Shit bitch, you got some good pussy." David yelled as he pulled out of her. She turned around and he stood there with his dick facing her looking at her. She knew what he wanted. She opened her mouth, and he slid his dripping wet dick inside of her mouth and she sucked it clean. He reached down and pulled his shorts back on. "Now, let's get down to business." He sat down next to her on the couch.

She didn't even bother to put on her jeans. She reached for her purse and grabbed the money from inside. "It's all there."

"For your sake, it better be." He grabbed the money and began to count.

Yvette laid back on the couch to collect her thoughts.

"It's all there Ma, and I'm in a good mood. Let's celebrate."

Yvette got up and bent down to retrieve her pants and panties. "Maybe another time. I really have a lot to do today."

David put the money down and looked at her

like she was crazy. "That wasn't a request, Ma. Leave those shorts off and take off that top. It's too damn hot in here for all of those clothes." Yvette wanted to cry. She realized that she had gotten in way over her head by reaching out to David. She could refuse and try to make a run for it, but she was half naked and what if she did make it? He still had those videos of her. She pulled her tank top over her head and took off her bra. She sat there naked waiting to see what he had in store for her.

David reached under the coffee table and produced a bottle of Hennessy. He opened it and took a long drink of it straight from the bottle. He handed it to Yvette. She shook her head in refusal and he stared at her. She took the bottle and turned it up to her lips. She took a swallow and began to choke. It was so strong. David laughed and took the bottle out of her hands. He pushed her back on the sofa and poured some on her nipples. She shuddered. He got on top of her and began to lick the brown warm liquid off of her nipples.

Yvette moaned and began to squirm. David really knew how to satisfy a woman. Too bad he was who he was. She would love to be able to get this on a daily basis.

She gasped as he started to play with her pussy. It was still tender and sore from their previous rough activities. David noticed her discomfort and stopped. "I see you are kind of tender down there."

She smiled and nodded. She rose up as he got up off of her. Feeling both disappointment and relief at the same time, she watched him as he disappeared down the hall and into the small bedroom she was in before.

He returned with a big jar of Vaseline. She looked at him curiously as he pulled down his shorts and scooped out some Vaseline and began to massage it onto his dick. When he got it all greasy, he walked over to her. "Bend over."

"David, I don't do that. I can't."

David kissed her, again, and gently rubbed her clit. His hand was still greasy, and it felt so good making her get wet all over again.

He stopped, picked up the bottle of Hennessy, turned it up to his mouth, and then put it to her lips. Yvette took a big gulp of the liquid and exhaled at the burning sensation she felt as it went down her throat. She grabbed the bottle and took another big sip. She was starting to feel the effects along with David playing gently with her tender pussy. She turned around and reached back and spread her cheeks.

"That's what I'm talking about, Ma." David pushed the head into her small tight anus. Yvette screamed out. David eased back. "Relax, Ma. Put your hand down there and play with that pussy." Yvette did as she was told, and he tried again. She cried out and David pulled back. He sat down on the couch and pulled her down with her back facing him. "I want you to sit on this dick while I finger your pussy. Relax, everything will be okay." Yvette's head was spinning, and she was so turned on when he started to finger her pussy.

She lifted up, grabbed his dick and placed it at the entrance of her asshole. She relaxed and pushed down on it. She lifted herself up and down trying to get the head of his dick into the opening. She was trying to concentrate, but it was hard because of the way he was playing with her pussy-- and the pain was excruciating. David lost his patience and grabbed her by her hips and pushed her downwards. She screamed as she felt his big dick pierce her asshole. The pain was like none she felt before in her life. She was too scared to move because she thought the huge dick would rip her hole. "Move your ass up and down on this dick. Why you just sitting there?"

Yvette took a deep breath and began to move up and down. The pain was unbearable.

David started playing with her pussy again, and it felt so good. She was experiencing both pain and pleasure and she loved it.

She began to move up and down at a faster pace and before she knew she was sitting all the way down on his dick. He was completely inside her. She started gyrating her hips and yelling out "Shit, David, this feels so good. I'm about to come!" She came so hard she started screaming "Yes!"

David held her up a few inches off his dick and started pumping up inside her ass. He moaned and pumped harder and harder. He lifted her up, with his dick was still inside her ass, and turned her face down on the couch. He grabbed her hips and proceeded to fuck her in the ass hard and steady. Yvette began to scream, moan, and cry. She didn't know if it hurt or if it felt good. She felt pressure in her ass, again, and realized she was about to come. She screamed at the top of her lungs.

David began to slap her on her ass hard and she felt like she was never going to stop coming. All of a sudden, he grabbed her hips and shoved his dick real hard all the way into her ass and held it there. "Bitch, I'm coming all in your ass."

Yvette couldn't move. She just put her face into the couch and whimpered. When he was done, he pulled out of her. She turned around and saw him standing there with his dick dripping with a mixture of sperm, blood and feces. Yvette looked alarmed. He looked at her and laughed. "Don't worry, Ma. I don't want you to eat your own shit. What kind of animal do you think I am?" He walked off to the bathroom and she heard him turn on the shower. He stuck his head out the bathroom door. "Hey, come get your nasty ass in this shower."

Yvette didn't really want to, but she knew she needed to clean up. She joined him in the shower and stood behind him.

He handed her the washcloth and stuck his soiled dick out to her. "Clean it." She obeyed. She noticed that as she began to wash it that it started growing again. When she finished, he grabbed her head and made her get on her knees while the water was running down on both of them and put it in her mouth. She sucked and gagged as he held her head and tried to force it down her throat. He let go of her head and let her go at her own pace for a while. He started moaning and grabbed her head again and began to shove it down her throat. He came in her mouth, and she swallowed every drop without gagging this time. She licked him clean. He let go of her head and smiled down at her. "You are one nasty, bourgeois bitch."

## 44

Sam waited patiently for Tessa to come out of the bedroom. He was worried about her, as she looked extremely tired when she answered the door. She ran down the details of what happened at her parent's house the night before, and it left him shocked and stunned. She wasn't quite dressed, and she asked him to sit and wait while she finished. Instead of going out, they opted to have take-out at her place so thcy could talk in private. He second guessed his decision to tell her his news, since she was still trying to process what she was told yesterday.

He was actually trying to process the whole thing himself. She finally came out of his room wearing some sweats-pants and a baggy tee-shirt that said *Pretty Plus* on the front. Her braids hung loosely down her back-- she looked so beautiful to him. He wanted to just put his arms around her and protect her, but he continued to set up the food he bought and pulled out the chair for her. For several minutes, they sat quietly and ate.

"Are your eggs okay, Tess?" She looked up at him and nodded, returning to eating her food. "I know this is hard for you to process, but I believe that they really had your best interest at heart when they made these decisions. I've been around both sets of parents and they are good people. They truly love you, especially Mr. Grant. He adores you, and anyone who is around you guys can see and feel it. As for the Duncans, I kind of understand in a way why he took me under his wing. I think he was trying to make up for not being able to be in your life."

"Even though I was a boy, I needed parents and he needed to feel good about the decision he made about you." Tessa looked up at Sam and laughed. "What's so funny?"

Tessa grinned widely at him. "I'm laughing because you are doing the very thing to me that I always do to you. Try to make you see the bright side of things and the good in every situation. I'm not laughing at what you said, because you made some good points. It's just weird how things just turned out. Me meeting you, your connection to my biological father, and you cheating with two sisters."

Tessa laughed again, although she could tell that Sam didn't think the last statement was very funny. "Come on, Sam. You have to admit, there is some humor in all of this." Sam smiled. He was glad he was able to make her smile. Tessa looked at him and frowned. "You're getting married Saturday."

Sam put his fork down. He guessed he would

have to discuss that situation today. "Actually, that's what I wanted to talk to about yesterday when I asked you to have dinner with me. I called off the wedding and the relationship, Tess. I had to finally be totally honest with you, Yvette, the Duncans, and myself. When I was digging into young Calvin's ass yesterday, I realized that I was not only talking to him, but myself, as well. I had been a selfish coward. I needed to do the right thing."

"I went to the Duncans and told them everything-- from the reason I went along with planning a marriage to their daughter even though I didn't love her, to my relationship with you. I even told them about how Yvette found out and what happened at the house."

Tessa looked down at her plate. "They told me that's how they found out about everything."

Sam nodded. "I guess I was the one who spilled the beans, although I didn't realize that I was opening up a whole can of worms. The truth just seemed to come out from everywhere."

"Yes, it did in a big way."

Sam scooted his chair over to the same side of the table as Tessa. "Tessa, I want to be there for you and our baby-- completely. I never felt this way about anyone in my life. When I first laid eyes on you, I knew that you were the one. When we ended things between us, I tried to stay away, but it hurt me like hell knowing that I was the reason you were hurting. I want my child to know their father, I want them to know that he loves their mother. I want our child to see what real love looks like, how a man and woman in love should treat one another, so they can know what to look for and how to treat the one that they fall in love with someday."

"Tessa, you can sit here and say you don't love me, but I refuse to believe that. I'm not trying to pressure you, but I don't feel like a man without you. I feel lost and incomplete. You are my rib, my heart, my soulmate. I know I will never find another woman like you. I know that I went about this the wrong way, but I will spend the rest of my life making it up to you. If you refuse me, I love you enough to stand back so that you can find your happiness, but I will still be a father to my child. You need to know that I will never stop wanting or loving you."

"I know things are crazy right now, but there's a reason for all of it. We will survive, and I want us to survive as a family. I know all of this is a lot and I will be patient, but all I ask for is a chance. I do want to marry you and I want us to be together forever, if you would just let me and give me a chance. We can go as slow as you want. The ball is totally in your court."

Tessa stared into Sam's eyes, thinking out her response to his confession. "Sam, I can't sit here and say that I have figured everything out, because I don't. All I know is that my world feels like a hurricane just blew in and I'm trying to find all of the pieces of my life, so I can put it back together. In these few months, I found out the two men in my life that I love are not who I thought they were. I found out I have a sister who hates me and probably would rather see me dead. I found out all of this, along with the fact that I'm actually bringing a child into this world of this craziness."

"I trusted you Sam, and you lied to me. I trusted my parents and they lied to me. I don't even know who to trust anymore. I feel like I don't know much of anything anymore. A part of me just feels like running away and never coming back, but that would be selfish to take my baby from their family. Last night, as I laid in bed, I kept hearing the voices of my parents, telling me their truth. My biological dad explaining himself, his wife's voice explaining to me, you apologizing for your actions, and Yvette calling me everything but my name. Then, the doctor congratulating me on my pregnancy. I actually had to put the pillow over my head to try to muffle out the voices, because I felt like I was going insane. That's not healthy for me or the baby. I have a lot of decisions to make and a lot to work out mentally."

"I know that I will not be left alone to do so, if I stay here in Richmond. I spoke with my doctor, and she said it would be okay for me to travel. I am booking a trip and going away for a few weeks to get my head straight before I end up in a mental institution or miscarrying. I'm not telling anyone where I'm going, but I will text you guys both when I arrive and from time to time to let you know that I'm doing okay. If I get sick, I will let you guys know, but I will be fine. My doctor has already connected me with her colleague where I'm going just in case anything happens."

"Tess, I don't want you to go, but I do want you to be healthy both mentally and physically for the sake of you and the baby. If you feel this is what's best, just tell me what you want me to do, and I will do it and respect your wishes."

Tessa hugged him and kissed him on the cheek. "Sam, I really do love you, but sometimes love isn't enough. I feel broken right now, and I just want to get back to being myself and be the best Tessa I can be. I need to do that so that I can be a great mom to our baby. "

Sam smiled at her-- this is why he loved her so much. "I'm glad to hear that, Tessa, and I know you want what's best for our baby. That's the least of my worries. I totally trust you as a mom." Tessa hugged and kissed him again. "I may not trust you in a relationship right now, but I do trust you as a dad." They stood up and held each other for a long time.

Tessa broke their embrace, and walked over to

her purse, and took out a set of keys. "These are the keys to the boutique. Angie will be in charge of everything when I'm gone. I don't want the renovations to be put on hold in my absence. She has all of my instructions on everything-- I'll be checking in daily with you guys about the shop. I do trust you with that."

They both laughed. "When will you be leaving?"

Tess sat on the couch and handed him some more paperwork about the boutique while answering. "In two days. I have a lot to do."

Sam put the papers on the counter and put his arms around her. "I'm going to miss you and the baby, Tess. Are you going to see your parents before you leave?"

Tessa laid her head on his chest and exhaled. He was really making this hard for her. A part of her almost asked him to come with her. "Yes, I owe them an apology for blowing up like I did. I love my parents and I know they love me. I may not like what they did, but I know they did it out of love, and I don't want to go out of town leaving things the way they are between us."

Sam held her tightly. He didn't want to let her go. "What about Ed?"

He felt her tense up a little "I was thinking about just sending him an email explaining how I feel right now. He is my biological father-- I don't want to come off as disrespectful or like I'm rejecting him. The fact that he knew so much about my life let me know that he really does care, and we can't change the past. I do want our baby to know all of its family."

"I think he would like that. He is really a good man. I hope you guys will be able to sort things out and develop a good relationship."

Tessa held on tighter to him. "Yes, me too. Now, my wonderful sister Yvette, that's another story. I don't want to begin to think about what can happen between me and her. I don't even want to talk about it right now."

Sam shook his head, "Me either, Tessa."

# 45

Yvette walked into the house that she and Charles once shared and looked around. She immediately noticed the *For Sale* sign in the yard and became angry. She dragged her sore body up the stairs as fast as she could. She needed to shower and change into something presentable to go meet with her parents.

Her head felt heavy from the effects of all of the Hennessy she had been drinking. Feeling nauseous, she ran to the bathroom and threw up. She had never had that type of alcohol. She was a champagne and wine type of girl.

She brushed her teeth and stepped into the shower to quickly wash her body. She dressed quickly in a royal blue halter jumper and some white sandals. She applied some makeup to cover up the dark circles that had formed under her eyes. She pulled her hair back into a ponytail and hurried out the house to go see her parents.

## 46

Ed and Margaret sat at the table and looked at their daughter eating like she hadn't eaten in years. This concerned them. "Vette, when was the last time you ate?"

Yvette looked up at her mom and put down her fork. "Mom, since Charles called off the wedding and left me, I haven't been able to eat or sleep. I feel like my world is crashing down around me. I just don't know what I did that was so wrong to make him treat me like this."

Yvette began to cry. Margaret walked over and placed her arms around her daughter, trying to console her. "Look, baby, this too shall pass. Some things just aren't meant to be. You have to move on and get your life in order."

Yvette laid her head on her mother's arm. "How am I supposed to do that? He put the house up for sale and when it's sold, I will have thirty days to move. I have no money coming in. He just left me out in the cold."

Ed looked at his daughter and was amazed at how different she was from Tessa. Nevertheless, maybe one day they could all get together and put all of this mess behind them. He knew that would take a whole lot of talking, healing, and time. "Vette, why don't you come back and live with us? But first, let me be clear-- it would only be for a couple of months. No more than three. This will give you time to get yourself together and figure out what you want to do with yourself. We know Charlie gave you some money, so that should hold you if you live here. It should be enough to help you get around to find a job or something."

Yvette smiled. "Thanks, Daddy!" She jumped up and gave him a big hug and kiss.

Ed smiled at his daughter "Now, don't think you're coming back in here to freeload. You can come and work at the office. I can find something for you to do while you're looking for work. You're 30-years-old and you need to be able to take care of yourself, girl. No free rides. If you were self-sufficient, no man would have been able to put you out of his home and up and leave you without any income. I hope you learned a lesson from all of this."

Yvette held her head down. "Yes, I sure did, Daddy. And don't worry, I'm going to do what I'm supposed to do and be out of here before you know it. I'm gonna make you both proud."

Margaret sat back down and looked at her daughter saying what she thought they wanted to hear. "I sure hope so, because from what we hear, you haven't exactly been making us proud with some of your actions. Yvette Margaret Duncan, how could you treat another woman the way you treated Tessa? I know your daddy and I didn't raise you to be so mean and conniving! And then you sat right in my face and lied to me about that dress! I know Charlie cheated on you, but what voice in your head told you to blame the other woman? She didn't even know about you! I am so embarrassed and disgusted by your behavior, girl! And let me tell you something else-- you need to watch how you treat folks, because you never know when you are going to cross their paths again or how it's going to affect your life! In other words, it will come back to bite you in your narrow ass!"

Ed sat quietly nodding in agreement with his wife. Yvette was speechless. "I'M TALKING TO YOU GAL! WHAT DO YOU HAVE TO SAY FOR YOURSELF AND YOUR UGLY BEHAVIOR?" Yvette and Ed jumped. They didn't expect Maggie to get loud.

Yvette looked frightened, but she knew she had better say something "Mommy, I was hurt and devastated. Here I was, planning this beautiful wedding for the man--"

Maggie banged the table, interrupting Yvette. "Girl don't try to feed me none of that pitiful bullshit. You strategically plotted and planned for that whole scenario to play out at that house. You humiliated that girl because you felt stupid, and you wanted her and Charlie to feel like you! Every time I think about what you did, I get sick to my stomach. And let me tell you something. You're going to pay us for not one, but both of those dresses!"

Yvette began to cry and looked at her mother in disbelief. *"How?"*

Maggie banged the table, once again "Figure it out! You have all the sense. You managed to come up with that scheme to bust them all by your little self. Now, figure out how to pay me and your Daddy back!"

Yvette sniffled and nodded. "Yes, ma'am."

Ed cleared his throat. He decided to go on to the difficult subject that they had been putting off. "Yvette, we have something else to discuss with you that you might find a little disturbing right now. But we need to tell you."

Yvette sighed. What else could it possibly be? She felt her stomach drop when she thought maybe David had sent those videos to them. Then again, she didn't really think it was possible because she would be laying on the floor. Her mother would have definitely stomped her into the floor and threw her out of the window by now. Just thinking about it sent chills down her spine.

"Baby, 35 years ago, before your mother and I got married or engaged, I got a woman pregnant in college and she had a daughter by me."

*"What?"*

"Gal, sit down and listen!" Yvette obeyed her mother and sat back down with tears rolling down her cheeks.

"Because of the circumstances, we all thought it would be better for the baby to be raised by her mother and her future husband at the time without her knowing who her biological father was. The woman and I were good friends, and we crossed the line one night, and she got pregnant. All of us-- your mother and I, the woman and her fiancé-- decided to let them raise the baby as their own and one day in the future reveal the truth if necessary. Given the events that have taken place these last few months, we decided that it was necessary to reveal the truth."

Yvette looked confused "So you're saying I have a half-sister?"

Ed nodded "Yes baby, you have a half-sister, and she lives in Richmond, and she is about to have a baby."

Yvette stomach was in knots. "Well, who is she?"

Ed cleared his throat. "You see, that's the thing your mother was talking about. How you treat people, and how you may cross paths again. Her name is Tessa Grant. The same Tessa Grant who owns Pretty Plus boutique in Richmond."

Yvette screamed and couldn't stop-- she wanted

to stop, but it was like she had left her body. Maggie jumped up and grabbed her daughter, slapping her across her face and grabbing her by the shoulders, shaking her hard.

Yvette broke away from her mother and turned to run towards the front door.

## 47

Yvette opened her eyes and saw her mother looking down at her with a worried look on her face. She turned her head, which was throbbing, and saw her father looking just as worried. She felt a cold cloth on her forehead. She tried to sit up, but the room began to spin. Her mother gently pushed her back "Lay back down, Vette. Don't try to move too fast."

Yvette obeyed her mother. "What happened?"

Maggie removed the cloth from her daughter's head. "You passed out, baby. You became hysterical and passed out."

It all came back to Yvette. She began to cry and tried to sit up again, and her parents stopped her. She looked around and realized she was in her old room. She turned her head away from them and started to cry.

Her father leaned down beside her and rubbed her cheek. "Baby, talk to Daddy. I need you to tell me how you feel about this."

Yvette kept her head turned away from her father. She did not want to speak to any of them. She knew she had to say something so they could leave her alone. "Daddy, I don't know how to feel right now. It's like everything is happening to me all at once. Can I just have some time to think and rest? I'm really tired."

Ed kissed his daughter on her cheek and stood up. "Okay, baby, I will let you rest. But we really do need to finish talking. I know this is a lot, but we have to deal with it so we can go on with our lives. I'm sorry for keeping it from you, but it doesn't change the fact that I love you all very much. Just like we expect you to take responsibility for your actions, I am taking responsibility for mine. You made a choice I don't agree with, and I made some you don't seem to agree with. At the end of the day, I'm still your father and still love you regardless of your choices."

Yvette rolled her eyes "But you're not just my father. I had to share you with Charles, and now you tell me there's someone else."

Margaret spoke up, "Yes, Yvette and you did not suffer one bit because of Charles's presence. If you hadn't done the things you have done, you wouldn't be so upset by the fact that Tessa is your sister. I'm going to give you a few days to let this entire situation sink in, and then you need to get up out of that bed and grow up. We need to figure out how to move forward as a family and act like we have some sense. And when I say family, I mean Tessa and her baby, too." Maggie kissed her daughter on her forehead and walked out arm in arm with her husband, leaving Yvette to her thoughts.

## 48

Sam and Rome walked into the house to meet the movers. They were there to remove the furniture from the house, as it was up for sale. He also wanted to get the rest of his personal belongings so he could move them to his apartment in Richmond.

When Sam and Rome stepped into the bedroom, the strong smell of bleach invaded their nostrils. When he walked into his closet, he couldn't believe his eyes-- there was bleach all over his designer suits and clothing.

Rome shook his head. "Man, that bitch is crazy, but I always told you that shit. Don't just stand there looking pissed. It could be a lot worse. You could have gone ahead and married the bitch."

Sam didn't say anything. He just walked back out of the closet and was about to sit on the bed until he realized that the mattress had several cuts all over it. "You know what, man? I guess I deserve all of this." He looked in the drawers and learned that his clothes in the drawers suffered the same fate as the ones in the closet.

"Damn," Rome mumbled.

Sam threw his hands up in frustration. "I give up. I can't deal with this right now. I'm about to call and tell the movers not to come. I'm going to get a cleaning crew to come in and try to clean and pack what's not damaged. Let's just go to every room to take an assessment of the damage."

Rome followed him out of the room. "Okay, you're the boss."

After about an hour, Sam came to the conclusion that he basically had nothing personal to move out of the house. So, he let the movers come and paid them extra to move everything out, including the items that were destroyed to dispose of them.

He couldn't even take his computer. It looked as if it had been beaten with a baseball bat. He kept all of his important paperwork at his office, so he didn't have to worry about that.

Tomorrow he would have some of his crew come to paint the walls and pull up the carpet that was destroyed. He wanted to get as much as he could on the sale of the house. In hindsight, Yvette did him a favor by destroying everything in the house. He actually didn't want anything that reminded him of that relationship.

Rome walked into the living room and interrupted his thoughts. "So, man, have you heard from Tessa?"

Sam smiled at the mention of her name. "Yeah, she called me this morning, letting me know that she was okay. She sounded relaxed and in good spirits." Tessa had been gone a week, but it felt like it had been a year to Sam.

"That's good, man. I'm really rooting for you two. If you mess this up again, I'm going to kick your ass!"

Sam laughed. 'I don't plan on messing up, man. I just hope she will take me back. But I'm going to be patient with her. I got some good people down there working on her shop. Even Calvin is doing a good job."

Rome nodded his head. "Yeah, he seems like a good kid. He reminds me of us when we were coming up."

Sam agreed. "Yeah, he does, and I want to make sure he gets a chance to make it just like we did-- so does Tessa." Sam closed the door to his former home and felt anxious and happy thinking about his future with Tessa.

## 49

Tessa walked along the beach of Key West, Florida at 6 am. It was so peaceful and pretty. The sound of the waves relaxed her, and the sand between her toes felt wonderful. This getaway was just what she needed to clear her mind. She spoke to Angie and Sam daily. There was just no way around it. They seemed to be working well together, getting the boutique renovated. That helped her to relax even more.

She had been in Florida for two weeks. She and Ed Duncan had been emailing each other every day. She hadn't planned to keep in contact with everyone so much, but it couldn't be avoided. They were worried about her, and she had to admit she enjoyed the love that she was receiving.

The original plan was for her to stay two more weeks, but she was getting homesick and decided to head back in a week. She had never taken a solo trip in her life before, and it was great. But it was time to go home and face the music. Ed and Maggie told her that Yvette knew about her now but didn't elaborate on her reaction. She decided not to stress it. She had time to think about things and had made some decisions.

She decided to let go of the anger she felt towards her parents and the Duncans. They made their decisions without malice in their hearts. Only love.

After communicating with the Duncans for the past few weeks, she could tell that they were good people. She felt lucky to have two sets of parents who loved her.

As for Sam, she couldn't deny the love and connection they had, even before the baby. She knew that no one was perfect, and she believed that he was the one for her. Tessa was willing to move forward with their relationship if he was willing to attend counseling with her. Her family dynamics were definitely going to affect their relationship, and both of them were going to need help dealing with it.

She looked out into the ocean and looked at the sunrise. When the baby kicked, Tessa giggled and rubbed her belly. "Don't worry, little one. We'll be heading home soon to be with your daddy and everyone who love us."

## 50

Ed was in the middle of reading an email from Tessa when Maggie walked in. "Hey, honey. Are you busy?"

Ed looked up from his computer and smiled at his wife. "No, just reading an email from Tessa. She says she will be coming home next week. She is getting homesick."

"It's about time," Maggie laughed. "Who knew she was going to skip town on us like that? I can't wait to see her. She's entering her sixth month. She really needs to be close to home, not off somewhere all alone."

Ed agreed with his wife. "I'm just so happy she is allowing us to be in her life. That reminds me-- I need to call Jeff to draw up some papers to get the trust fund started for the baby."

Maggie held up her hand. "I already took care of that."

Ed smiled at his wife. He adored her. "That's why I keep you around, gal. You know how to handle business in more ways than one." He smiled and winked his eye at her. Maggie rolled her eyes and pretended to be mad but couldn't hold in her laughter.

"All jokes aside, honey, we need to do something about Vette."

Ed became serious and frowned. "What do you mean? She's been coming in here working every day, and I've seen her going out to interviews."

Maggie stood up and started straightening up Ed's messy desk. "That's what I mean. She gave in too easily, and she's very quiet. She hasn't made one mention of how to reconcile with Tessa, nor has she sat down at the dinner table with us one time." Maggie started cleaning up Ed's mess. "Ethel has been taking her meals up to her."

"Well, has she mentioned anything to Ethel?"

Maggie sat back down. "No, but Ethel said she walked in to bring her meal to her last night, and she could hear Vette in the bathroom crying. She knocked on the door to find out if she was okay, but Vette told her she was fine and that she wasn't crying. Ethel left her plate in the room and left. Ethel agrees that something is not right with her."

This concerned Ed. He was so wrapped up in the happiness he felt about Tessa that maybe he dropped the ball on paying attention to how all of this was affecting his other baby girl. Who said being a parent was easy, even after they were grown? "When she comes into the office tomorrow, I'm going to take her shopping and out to lunch and have some daddy/daughter time with her. I will try to pick her brain. Shopping always makes her happy."

Maggie narrowed her eyes. "Okay, but don't overdo it, Eddie. I know our baby, and she's a slick, manipulative one. I just want her to be a responsible adult and a good person. And I guess we are partly to blame. We spoiled her, trying to overcompensate for our guilt about Tessa. We were focusing on making sure she had all of the things she wanted, neglecting to give her some of the things that she needed. We ended up spoiling her, and now she feels as if the world revolves around her. So, trust me. She is not going to welcome Tessa with open arms. Nor is she happy that she is not the only child." Ed knew his wife was right, but he still wanted to spend some time with Yvette. "Why isn't she working today?"

Ed got up and put on his jacket, and grabbed his briefcase. "She had two interviews!" Maggie gave him the side eye, but she didn't respond. He knew what that look meant, and he smiled and escorted her out of his office. "Come on, honey. Let me take you out to dinner".

## 51

Yvette took the blunt from David and put it to her lips. She took a long pull. She relaxed as she felt the effects of the powerful weed do its job. She lay naked next to David in his tiny bedroom. Lately, she had been hanging out with him at least once a week. She realized he was the only one who understood her feelings towards Tessa and Charles. She also loved the sex. She thought it was out of this world. She didn't mind taking the drive. It was worth it to escape being around her fake parents. She actually liked hanging out at this run-down house.

The only drawback was that David was unemployed and broke. She found herself always having to fund their little *'parties'* by stopping at the ABC store and different restaurants to get Hennessy and takeout every time she visited. They definitely needed food; the hunger was something serious after smoking weed.

David was lying next to her naked, stroking her inner thigh. They were both intoxicated but felt mellow and relaxed. "I still can't believe you and Tessa are sisters--"

"Half-sisters." Yvette corrected him.

David laughed. "My bad. You need to stop tripping and get back on your people's good side so you can get your funds back up, Ma."

Yvette turned the bottle of Hennessey up to her mouth. She had gotten used to the taste. "I'm never going to accept that bitch and her bastard child as my family. What we need to do is figure out a way to get some money together. Maybe you can pay someone to set my car on fire. Then I can collect the insurance money."

David moved his hand up to her nipple, ran his finger over it, and started rolling it between his fingers. "Nah, it's not worth it. You need a hustle that will get your income rolling in consistently. You need to hook up with one of those square-ass rich niggas. Fuck and suck his brains out to make him fall in love and wife you. You can do that or get your daddy to hook you up with a high-paying gig. Use that degree your parents spent all that money on."

Yvette moaned, enjoying what he was doing to her nipple. "How am I going to do that? I can't even show my face at the country club or dinner parties after the way Charles embarrassed me. And I really don't want to work. My parents have money."

"I'm telling you that's what you need to do." David laughed. "Get your people to hook you up. Tell 'em you ready to move on. I'm sure some of their rich friends have some rich, lonely square-ass sons. Your parents already made it clear that they are not gonna take care of your lazy ass."

Yvette reached down and grabbed David's dick and started to stroke it. "They don't care about me. All they care about is that bitch-- when she's coming back to town, how her store is shaping up, and how she will be back in business in no time."

David pulled her on top of him. He grabbed her ass cheeks and squeezed them, "Tessa be making moves though, and she knows how to get that paper. Not only is she about her paper, but her head game was also tight, and she had some good pussy to be a big girl".

Yvette jumped up and looked around for her clothes. "So, you're a fan of hers, too? Well, I'll just leave so you can jack off and reminisce about her sucking your dick!"

David looked at her and smiled. "Ma, get your little ass back in this bed and stop trippin." Yvette crossed her arms, pouted, and crawled back into the bed. "You are one crazy bourgeois bitch, you know that? But I like it. Now let's get back to how you gonna get your paper up."

Yvette went back to playing with his dick. David rubbed her ass and stuck his finger between her cheeks, sliding his finger in her ass. Yvette moaned and stuck her ass out, giving him more access. "I won't be able to do anything with that bitch in the way. I'm telling you they already set up a trust fund for that baby, and now they're planning this huge baby shower for when she returns. We need her out of the way, David."

David began thinking about how his life took a turn for the worse after Tessa had him arrested, and how he should be the one standing by her side, living off that money she makes from the boutique. He felt his anger rise. "When did you say she's coming back?"

Yvette smiled. "Next Friday. Charles is supposed to pick her up from home to keep her busy until the baby shower starts."

Yvette started licking the head of his dick. David moaned. "Climb up on this dick and let's make some plans for some get back."

Yvette smiled and stood over him with each of her legs on his sides. She squatted down and moaned as she lowered her pussy onto his dick. She felt happier than she felt in months. She was about to get back at all of them and no one had any idea what was about to happen.

## 52

Sam was frustrated. His former neighbor left a message with his secretary saying his sprinklers had been on nonstop for the past 3 days. Now he had to leave his office and drive 45 minutes to the house to turn off the sprinklers and then rush to Richmond in order to pick up Tessa by 2:00. He also had to keep her busy until the baby shower started. It seemed like everything that could go wrong, was going wrong today.

When he pulled up to the house, the front yard was almost flooded. "Shit! What next?" He walked up to the house and unlocked the door. He walked through the house, into the garage, turned off the sprinklers, and dismantled the wires.

He walked back through the now-empty house while pulling out his phone to call Tessa to let her know he was running late. She picked up after the second ring. "Hey, baby, I'm running a little behind. I had to stop at the house and take care of an issue."

"Is everything okay?"

Sam walked up to the door and realized he left his keys on the workbench in the garage. He turned around and headed back to the garage. "Yeah, the sprinkler system is malfunctioning. I dismantled the wires, but the yard is a mess."

Before Tessa could respond, he noticed Yvette standing in the middle of the living room. "Um, Tessa let me call you back when I'm on my way."

Tessa was concerned again. "Are you okay?"

Sam responded slowly. "I'm fine. I just need to take care of something else right quick."

Tessa wasn't convinced, but she let it go. "Okay, baby. Love you."

Charles looked at Yvette as he responded to Tessa. "I love you too. I'll see you soon." He disconnected the call and stood looking at Yvette. She had no makeup on, and she looked tired and worn. "What are you doing here?"

Yvette smiled and walked over to Sam. "Is that how you greet your ex-fiancé and aunt to your child, Charles? Or should I call you Sam?" Sam was really getting annoyed. He had no time for Yvette and her bullshit today. "The neighbor called me about the sprinklers and said he couldn't get in touch with you."

Sam started walking towards the door in an effort to get rid of her. "Well as you can see it's been taken care of and I would appreciate it if you hand over those keys. This is not your property."

Yvette laughed "What's wrong? You scared you're going to be late picking up your baby mama?"

Sam was losing his patience. "Yvette, what do

you want from me, more money?"

Yvette rolled her eyes. "Do you see all this shit you created running to my parents whining to them about our relationship? You opened up this big ass can of worms and turned my life upside down. You could have come to me like a man and told me you wanted to end it-- but *no*, you had to go crying like bitch and put our business in the streets. Then you topped it off by getting this bitch pregnant! And what did I get? A check and kicked out into the streets."

Sam shook his head in disbelief. "Yvette, I never realized how delusional you were up until now. If I had come to you and told you how I felt you wouldn't have let it drop just like that. You and I both know it. Again, I apologize for how things turned out. I know this is a difficult time for you, but we have to live in our truths in order to be happy."

Yvette snorted at his statement and clapped. "Bravo for Charles Samuel Thompson and him living in his truth. Well, while you're so busy living in your *truth*, Mr. Perfect, how about adding this to it and see how happy this will make your baby mama." Yvette reached into her purse and threw a plastic stick wrapped in a piece of paper at him. Sam let it fall to the floor at his feet and looked down at it curiously. Yvette laughed, "Go ahead, pick it up, *Mr. Truth.*" Sam bent down and picked up the object and unwrapped the paper from around the stick. When he looked at both the paper and the stick, he felt as if the wind had been knocked out of him.

Yvette stood with her hands on her hips with an evil smirk on her face. "That's right, read it and weep, Player! I'm pregnant with your baby."

# 53

The doorbell woke her up.

Tessa must have dozed off while she was waiting for Sam to call her back. She got up from the couch, walked to her door, and swung it open, a large smile stretched across her face. "You finally made it." Her smile quickly faded when she realized it wasn't Sam.

"Hey, Ma. Long time no see." Tessa stood face-to-face with her ex.

"David."

Loved what you read?
Want more?
Enjoy the rest of the
five-part series,
*Truth and Lies*
by Demetrice Nichele.


Part 1 *When the Truth is a Lie*
Part 2 *Living in the Truth*
Part 3 *When the Truth Won't Set You Free*
Part 4 *Living the Lies*
Part 5 *Demise of the Lies*

*More coming soon...*

# ABOUT THE AUTHOR

Demetrice Nichele has been writing short stories, plays, and novels since she was in grade school. Her passion for storytelling is felt through her ability to paint the intricate and sometimes messy lives of everyday people on the page.

Demetrice is the mother of two adult children. When not writing, she enjoys serving customers in her baking business, reading, traveling, and cooking.